I1988539

Greenhorn Doc

Young Potterson, an erstwhile Scottish medical student, had been sent to America in disgrace. Now he found himself the owner of a wagon filled with Dr Markham's Elixir of Life, a dubious concoction guaranteed to cure any ailment known to mankind.

But when he was attacked by Indians, Potterson's introduction to the untamed West began in a far bloodier fashion than he could ever have imagined. Soon, too, he would face hostile guns with death never far away.

Would the Greenhorn Doc finally make out or would he be yet another victim of knife or bullet?

Greenhorn Doc

TEX LARRIGAN

A Black Horse Western

ROBERT HALE · LONDON

© Tex Larrigan 2004
First published in Great Britain 2004

ISBN 0 7090 7489 1

Robert Hale Limited
Clerkenwell House
Clerkenwell Green
London EC1R 0HT

Typeset by
Derek Doyle & Associates, Liverpool.
Printed and bound in Great Britain by
Antony Rowe Limited, Wiltshire

ONE

Jimmy Shakeshaft gripped the reins of his restless horse tightly with one hand while he raked
the valley below through army glasses. The scene
was familiar even though he hadn't visited the
Indian village since the day he'd ridden in and
found the totem pole standing upright in the
middle of what had once been his wife's tepee.
The totem was dedicated to the fire god, who
had taken Kalia and his son from him and was
supposed to keep the two spirits from returning
to haunt those who'd condemned Kalia and the
boy to die because she was the wife of a man
tainted with white man's blood.

He'd gazed long and hard while the
Cheyenne braves crowded around him, frightened of the big army repeating rifle that he
carried in a holster at the animal's shoulder.

He blamed himself for what had happened.
He should never have left the girl to go and

scout for the 'White-eyes'. He should never have listened to her pleas to stay with her tribe. She would be safe with them, she'd said. That had been the mistake. He should have taken them both to the fort where he was stationed, even though squaws were looked down on. At least she would be alive today, he thought bitterly.

It was seven years since that dreadful day when he'd turned his back and ridden away without saying a word. The crowd had been silent and sullen as they watched him go, safely, because Kalia's father had decreed it. He was Chief Black Bear of that particular tribe of Cheyenne.

Now he was sitting watching the comings and goings of those left in the permanent winter village. They seemed to be only old men and women and children down there. He had a great decision to make. He could go on down there and warn them that the white soldiers were coming in revenge for an attack by Cheyenne braves two weeks ago; the massacre of seven women and children and two old men could not go unpunished. He, as chief scout for the army at Fort Blaine, had followed the spoor of the raiding party and saw them heading for this particular village with concern.

He knew the procedure. The young braves would first clean up and purify themselves, then proclaim their deeds and prowess to the elders of the tribe; then would come the celebration and the dancing after the sun had gone down.

He knew he had two choices. He could wheel his horse about and go hell for leather back to the patrol out seeking the raiders, or he could go down and warn the Cheyenne that the white soldiers were coming.

He cursed. There were those down there who were his blood relatives, though he had never been shown kindness by any but his own mother. He'd been shunned because he had white man's blood in him, but he and his mother had been saved by the strength of will of a man willing to take as wife a squaw who had been raped by a white man. The man, Shakeshaft by name, had treated him as his own son, and saved him from much vicious treatment when he was a child. But Shakeshaft stopped an army bullet when Jimmy was in his teens. Before his death he had advised Jimmy to leave the village and go and seek his father at Fort Blaine. That had been twenty years ago.

Jimmy Shakeshaft's face tightened when he remembered his first encounter with the sergeant who was his father. Jimmy had been a naïve youth who had thought he would be welcome when he offered to Sergeant Jock Willis the token that the sergeant had given Jimmy's mother more than fifteen years ago. Willis had laughed, looked him up and down and then spat on the parade ground.

'You don't look like me, son, but you sure have grey eyes. You're a halfbreed, allright. Whether you're mine is another matter but you're welcome to stick around. You can tell us all you know about those Indian bastards!'

He'd been conscious of curious glances and hostility from those crowding about him. He was getting the same contemptuous treatment from them as he had from the Cheyenne!

The realization burned into his soul, but he only smiled and said nothing.

It was easy to talk about the Cheyenne, their ways and their movements. He felt no loyalty to those who'd treated him ill. It was only later when he met Kalia that his heart softened towards his mother's people.

He was tough. He learned to live alongside his father's people. He became a scout because he knew the terrain. Later when war came, he was raised to chief scout with several scouts working with him as a team.

It was just before the War between the States, in which white men fought white men, that he married Kalia. That was his happiest time, but when his company was withdrawn from Fort Blaine to go and fight the Rebels he'd made the worst decision of his life. Kalia had gone back to her village.

Jimmy's mount sidestepped, prancing a little, tail waving, and ears pricked.

'Whoa, there, girl,' he muttered softly. 'What's the matter with you?' He patted her neck to calm her down.

The mare leapt aside as if a snake had risen up in front of her. That movement saved his life as a knife came whizzing from the undergrowth behind him and thunked into a dead tree-trunk. Jimmy's reaction was instinctive. He was out of the saddle in an instant, turning to face his enemy in a crouch, his own knife in one hand.

He saw Swift Deer, a brave he'd known as a youth come hurtling at him, snarling, his lips drawn back, teeth bared and a tomahawk raised to strike him down. The two men closed with each other like two stags locking horns, then came the silent struggle. Both men were well-muscled and fit and each used every trick of close combat to outdo the other.

Jimmy's grip on Swift Deer's knife-wielding wrist gradually tightened until the knife fell from nerveless fingers. Swift Deer howled a cry of rage as he gripped Jimmy's head and scrabbled for his eyes. Both men's legs kicked and twisted around like a nest of serpents attacking each other.

Jimmy kicked out blindly, blood now pouring from his nose as he groped for Swift Deer's topknot of hair. His fingers felt the shaven head, then grasped the long scalplock and jerked the man's head sharply backwards. Swift Deer gurgled. In that moment Jimmy aimed a blow with the side of his other hand at the brave's exposed throat.

He felt the strength drain away from the Indian, who crumpled and lay still. Jimmy wiped blood from his eyes, struggled to his feet and then stood panting, looking down at the man who'd once been a member of the gang who'd tormented him in his youth.

He felt no remorse, only a cold feeling of relief that it was all over. He dragged the body into the bushes and left it without another thought. A hot rage was enveloping him. Those bastards down there had still not forgotten that by marrying him, one of their own women had been sentenced to death along with her child. The feud between them was as fresh today as it had been seven years ago.

His decision was made. He would return to Lieutenant Somerville out there somewhere on patrol and report his find. If they attacked soon, they would catch the raiders during their celebrations. The young braves would be drunk and they wouldn't know what hit them. As for the women and children . . . Jimmy Shakeshaft knew it wasn't the policy of the army to kill non-hostiles.

He mounted up, wheeled his horse and trotted away in the direction he'd last glimpsed the horse patrol.

*

Lieutenant Somerville raised an arm and pulled up his horse. The patrol behind him stopped too. Sergeant Gilroy moved his mount up beside the officer.

'Something wrong, sir?'

'Nothing I know of, Sergeant. I'm wondering where the hell Shakeshaft is. He should have reported back by now. We'll take a break. My ass is getting blisters. Give the order to stand down.'

'Yessir!' Abe Somerville smiled to himself at the enthusiasm old Gilroy showed. The poor old fellow should have retired years ago!

He swung off his horse as the sergeant bellowed his order which was repeated by a corporal further down the line. The men were exhausted with the gruelling routine of riding day after day looking for the renegade Cheyenne who'd massacred the women and children in the small settlement back near the fort.

Abe Somerville stretched and groaned, his back ached and his stomach growled for some real food. He could have given his eye-teeth for a juicy steak and some hash browns but all the cooks could come up with on patrol was dry bread and over-salted belly of pork. He spat in the dust. He'd be goddamned glad to get back to the fort and he wished Shakeshaft would move his ass and come back with some real information. The men were restless and vengeful. All had been shocked at the sight of the mutilated bodies.

The camp was soon set up. Lieutenant Somerville was proud of his men and their usual discipline. They were a cheerful bunch as a rule, but now there was an air of brooding moodiness about them which he didn't like. It was going to take all his experience and willpower to keep them in hand.

They didn't know it, but he was aware of their mutterings. The younger men were for going on the rampage, seeking out any redskin and carrying out a killing spree. They didn't like this day after day following the tracks of the raiders who had the know-how to cover up their trail. It took a man like Shakeshaft, who was part Cheyenne himself, to follow and report back when they eventually reached their hideout.

Now they could only wait, rest and eat, clean their weapons and be ready to ride.

After the meagre meal was finished the man on look-out gave a shout,

'Rider coming in, sir, at a hell of a lick!'

Somerville came swiftly out of his small tent to wait and watch for the newcomer. He hoped to God it was Shakeshaft with good news.

The rider didn't pull up until he was only yards from the officer's tent, then he did so with a jerk of the reins, so that the mare reared on her hind legs, causing a hell of a dust. Trust Shakeshaft to make a grand entrance, thought the lieutenant sourly. He was a show-off bastard.

Shakeshaft sprang down from the mare, gave her a pat on the head, then strode over to the officer. He did not salute. He'd always made it quite plain to Somerville that as he wasn't a recruited soldier, but only a scout, he had no allegiance to the army as such. They paid him for his services only and he didn't kowtow to anybody.

His manner was always that of an equal.

'Well? Did you track the bastards?' Somerville's voice was brusque. He valued Shakeshaft as a scout but he never forgot he was a 'breed.

'Yes, Lieutenant. They're holed up in a village beyond the mountains. A four-hour ride through the pass. The trail's too rough for wagons. You'll only get through on horseback. Every man will have to take rations and enough ammo for several days. There's no knowing whether they'll have left the village when we get there. We might have to track 'em again.'

'Right! Thank you, Shakeshaft. We'll move out at dawn. You look as if you could do with a good night's sleep!'

Shakeshaft smiled wryly. That was putting it mildly. He needed food and a bath and a chance to check on the sticky bloody wound in his arm,

13

which throbbed alarmingly.

Somerville watched him go to the chuck wagon, limping a little. The man was a tough customer. A pity he was a 'breed. He could have made a friend of him.

He called Gilroy, who'd been hovering nearby, and gave the orders for the dawn start. There was to be no late-night gambling and telling yarns around the camp-fires tonight. It would be bed down and get as much rest as possible. Tomorrow could be another harrowing day.

The route of Shakeshaft's headlong flight, which had taken him four hours to cover, stretched into twenty-four for the patrol. The men grumbled. The cooks had been left behind and they had to shift for themselves. They were beset by fleas and insects and some suffered from itchy sweat rashes. Their beards had grown long and they all smelled like pig's droppings.

At last they camped some way from the mountain village and Shakeshaft took Somerville and Gilroy to the high point where he'd hidden to watch the village.

'That's their home village, Lieutenant. Their tracks led straight there. I did some reconnoitring before reporting back. They're there, unless of course, they've planned another raid.'

Somerville looked at him curiously.

'Is there something the matter, Shakeshaft? You sound reluctant to talk about them.' He

14

raked the village with his glasses and saw the peaceful scene of women about their cook-fires and children playing. 'I don't see many menfolk around.'

'That's because they'll have been sleeping off their celebration of the success of the raid.'

'You think that, Shakeshaft?'

'Yes. You see, that was my village when I was young. I know how they go about things. The young men go out hunting, count coup and come back and boast about their prowess. They prove themselves as fit warriors. Those raiders who killed those women and children were young men counting coup. They will have "earned their spurs", to use a white man's term.'

Somerville studied him shrewdly.

'You've got no love of that village. Why?'

Shakesaft shrugged. 'They treated me like a pariah dog because of my tainted blood. It was only because I was protected by my mother's husband that I lived. When he lay dying because of a white man's bullet, he told me to leave the village for my own safety. I did so, leaving my mother behind. Later, I heard that she was starved to death, not allowed any food and no help from the womenfolk. She died an outcast because she had been raped by a white man.' He stopped abruptly and then said shortly, 'But you don't want to hear the rest.'

'But I do. I'm sorry, Shakeshaft, that you had

15

an unhappy start to your life. It makes me understand you better. I didn't have a good childhood myself.'

Shakeshaft drew a deep breath.

'You might as well know the rest. Several years later, I met Kalia at the fort. She was young and beautiful. We fell in love and we vowed to live together for ever. We had a child . . . a son and we were happy. Then when the war came, I volunteered as a scout. To me it was no different scouting against rebel Indians from scouting for white men against white men. Kalia wanted to go back to her village . . . our village. I wanted her to stay in the fort but the white women made her life miserable. She wanted to go home where she said she would be safe amongst her own people. I let her go, promising to come back for her when the war was over. I did so.

'I kept my promise and was looking forward to us being together again and to seeing my son. But she was dead, and my son too, Lieutenant. Can you understand people who turn on their own flesh and blood? They imprisoned them in her tepee and fired it as a token to the Fire God because she slept with a man who had white blood in his veins! It was my fault. I should never have allowed her to return, not after the treatment my mother got!'

Somerville put a hand on Shakeshaft's arm.

'Don't blame yourself, Shakeshaft. You couldn't have known.'

'I *should* have known! Do you know what it's like to be shunned both by your father's people and your mother's?' There was raw anguish in Shakeshaft's voice.

'So that's why you didn't hesitate to come back here and report the location of the raiders?'

'Yes!' The word was uncompromising. 'I'm still a hunted man. One of the young men who used to tease and bully me was one of the lookouts. He saw me and recognized me. I saw the hate in his eyes as we wrestled together before I killed him. He called me by name and he died cursing me!'

'You didn't report the incident, Shakeshaft!'

'No. It was a private matter.'

'Will there be others out there on the watch?'

'Yes. I'll show you their outposts at daybreak and we can outflank them and close in before they can sound the alarm. I want all the bastards caught, Lieutenant.' His voice was low and vicious.

Somerville shivered. He'd rather have Shakeshaft as a friend than an enemy. He was very much an animal on the prowl.

Daybreak came and all seemed quiet. Shakeshaft quietly pointed out the crags of rock to Somerville and Gilroy where the lone sentries would be posted. Two soldiers skilled in woodcraft were sent to each outpost to take care of the unsuspecting braves.

Then the men walked their horses, holding on to rattling bridles, as they closed in on the sleeping village. The men were ready and eager to take the village by storm.

Somerville ordered Gilroy to take his troop to spread out and surround the village; he would do likewise and on the first shot the attack would begin.

Shakeshaft's heart beat fast as he took in the familiar sight of the village. It was just the same as it had been all those years ago. The cooking-fires were burned down, logs piled beside the glowing embers ready for the morning's cooking ritual. Iron pots were at the ready, cornmeal soaking, ready to be boiled up to mush. He knew the routine. Soon the womenfolk would be coming out to start the day's work.

He glanced at Somerville.

'The men have their orders about the women and children?'

'Yes, I gave strict orders to spare them and the old men. We white men don't fight innocent women and children!'

'Good. I wanted to be sure!'

A woman emerged from her tepee just as the first shot came. She screamed and dived back inside the tent. Then there was a pounding of horses' hoofs as the troop rode in, firing into the tepees as they came.

The Indian warriors erupted from the tents, howling and screaming, firing old muskets as they came, then throwing them away and leaping up to unhorse a passing trooper. Some succeeded but others were shot at close quarters, their screams mingling with the shots and yells of the troopers who'd suddenly gone mad with blood-lust.

Bodies strewed the ground, bluecoats as well as half-naked Indians. Those troopers still on horseback lunged and cut at the knife-wielding braves. Blood spurted on to horses' necks, the sickly smell sending the animals into a panic.

The air was filled with smoke from firearms; the stench of gunpowder and blood was overpowering.

Gilroy's throat was slashed by a knife as he bent over his horse's neck to shoot a brave wielding a tomahawk. He never saw the assailant who threw the knife.

The lieutenant aimed and fired until his gun was empty, then he lunged and slashed at the oncoming Indians until his sword dripped with blood.

Suddenly it seemed to be over. Few screaming braves were left and those who were still alive were soon dispatched. Then the screaming started and Somerville was horror-stricken to see a group of his men dragging out women from the tepees while the children were throwing stones and attacking the troopers with sticks to ward them off.

'Stand down, you men!' roared Somerville. 'Your orders are to leave the women and children alone!' But his voice went unheeded. Shakeshaft was nowhere in sight, only his corporal and the young bugler were at hand.

He turned to the white-faced young bugler, a boy of sixteen.

'Sound the retreat, mister! I want every one of those men put under arrest for disobeying orders!'

The bugle did not sound. Somerville turned sharply to see what was causing the delay and saw the boy's eyes staring blankly. His jaw had dropped open and he was slowly slumping forward in his saddle. A knife was sticking out of his back and a youth of about ten was crawling away in the long grass.

Without thought, Somerville charged at him and trampled him to death under his horse's feet. Then he closed his eyes. What in hell had he become? He was no better than the men who'd dragged out the women and killed them.

He drove his horse to the nearest fire. He bent over, pulled a partly burned tree-branch from the embers and waved it over his head until it blazed up. Then he raced to the nearest tepee and flung it inside the opened flap. Soon smoke and flames leapt high into the air.

The men cheered and did likewise until the whole village was burning. Then he rode amongst his men, looking grim.

'If there are women left alive, let them go! We're not here to fight innocents!'

'They started it,' yelled one trooper. 'I saw a woman kill Jackson and another attacked my mate, Sorenson and the youngsters came at us like a swarm of locusts! They deserve to die!'

'I said, let them go, trooper! You will report to the guardhouse when we return to Fort Blaine!'

'Like hell I will!' yelled the angry man. The rest of the platoon listened silently to the tirade, and then looked at the lieutenant for his reaction. It soon came.

Somerville snatched the corporal's army gun from its holster and without a word, shot the trooper in the chest. Then coolly he looked about him.

'Anyone else shares that trooper's views?'

Without a word the men turned away. Those who were holding a bunch of women and children prisoner reluctantly let them go. Their lieutenant was proving himself a strong, fearsome leader, a man whom they could respect. Somerville glanced at Corporal Myers, still angry.

'See to it, Corporal! Put a guard on those women and children and get a party organized to pick up our dead and wounded, and Corporal . . .'

'Sir?'

'Get your priorities right! You can't hunt with both the fox and the hounds, not if you want to become sergeant!'

'Yessir!' Corporal Myers saluted, stiffened his back and moved off, bellowing as he went.

'Fall in, A Troop, at the double! Round up the wounded and the dead! B Troop, take over guard duties for the prisoners and C Troop, guard the perimeter of the village against attack! Anything else, Lieutenant?'

Somerville slapped his thigh with his gauntlets.

'That's it, Corporal. You're doing fine. Keep this up and I'll recommend you for sergeant!'

'Very good, sir.' Myers went proudly down the lines of men to see that his orders were carried out.

Somerville looked around for Shakeshaft. Where the hell was the fellow? He'd not seen him since the thick of the fighting. It was as if he'd disappeared when all hell broke out when the men attacked the women.

His eyes raked a stand of trees close by. His keen sight revealed a flicker of movement amongst the thick foliage. Curious, he took a walk and there he found Shakeshaft sitting cross-legged facing east. It looked as if this strange fellow was actually meditating. For a moment Somerville watched him silently, then he coughed. It was as if Shakeshaft came back from a far distance.

'What are you doing, Shakeshaft? There's a lot of clearing up to do out there!'

'Not my duty, Lieutenant,' Shakeshaft drawled. 'I have other things on my mind.'

Somerville felt anger rise within him.

'You go out of your way to remind me you're a civilian. Why do you do this?'

Shakeshaft shrugged. 'I am a free spirit. I do what I'm paid for and no more. You forget, those people were once my people. Would you not distance yourself if the roles were reversed?'

Somerville leaned up against a tree and looked down at the sitting figure.

'Where will it all end, Shakeshaft? You belong nowhere. Have you no friends?'

'No, Lieutenant, unless I can call you friend.'

Somerville nodded. 'I like to think I can rely on your loyalty. I suppose that's friendship.'

'I guess so. I feel loyalty to you but not to the colonel back at the Fort. He is just a representative of the government that pays me. If you were killed in battle, Lieutenant, I should not think twice about absconding and the colonel could go to the devil and take his garrison with him!'

'Huh! You'd better not repeat those remarks to anyone else!'

'You think I'm a fool?'

'Never a fool. Shakeshaft, never that!'

Somerville was to think back about that conversation when they eventually returned to Fort Blaine. Colonel Bathurst was furious at the report about the attack on the non-hostiles.

'Goddammit, Somerville, can't you control your troops? What in hell is going to happen when the Cheyenne hear of the massacre of those women and children . . . nine women and five children and two old men before you could stop the carnage? We could have a major uprising again! Those devils are uneasy and they don't need an excuse to start up the war drums! Holy Mary! We haven't enough men to hold out for a month if they get organized! There's our women and children to think of.'

'Sir! The men were horrified at the massacre at Sutton Springs. We were on the march for more than a week before Shakeshaft found the raiders' bolthole. We took revenge, sir. We killed all the band and it was the women and kids who started on our troopers. Before I knew what was happening, the men took revenge. There was no stopping them for a time!' He paused and then said quietly, 'They were like animals, sir. You want to be out there and experience hand to hand fighting yourself, sir! It is easy to get carried away!'

'Are you condoning what happened, Lieutenant?'

'No, sir, just trying to explain.'

'I'm surprised at you, Somerville. I think you're weak and your loyalties lie in the wrong direction. I'm putting you under arrest for inciting rebellion!'

'But, sir . . .'

'Not another word!' The colonel glanced at the captain who was sitting at a desk in the corner of the office taking notes. 'Take him to the guardhouse, Villiers, where he will stay until we can arrange a court martial!'

Stunned, Somerville glanced from one to the other. Then he stood up stiffly, saluted and left the room. It was the end.

TWO

Shakeshaft was lounging on the veranda of the bunkhouse assigned to the six scouts, drinking rotgut whiskey and listening to the latest scandal told with much gusto by one of the other scouts.

'. . . and there she was, as cheeky as you like, all spread out with skirts above her waist, and she an officer's wife, supposed to be a one-time prissy schoolmarm and her fornicating with a goddamn private! Granted her husband is twenty years older than her but you'd think at least she'd do it with an officer! It just goes to show them hoity-toity stuck-up women are no different from the trollops in the cathouses! In my opinion all women are trollops. What do you think, Shakeshaft?'

But Shakeshaft didn't hear the question. He was sitting up and frowning as he stared across the parade ground at the two men coming out of the colonel's office. What in hell was Somerville

26

doing being escorted all stiff and proper by Captain Villiers, the colonel's aide, and, what was worse, they were heading for the guard-house!

'Well? What d'you think, Shakeshaft?' But Shakeshaft brushed the question aside and stood up.

'I'll see you around, Pete. I've got something urgent to see to.' He moved off across the open space. Pete spat on to the ground.

'He's a moody bastard,' he said to the other men listening to him. 'You never know where you are with him!'

Shakeshaft slowed to a lounging walk, eyes on the two men. He'd guessed right. They made for the guardhouse. The trooper on duty saluted the captain and allowed them inside after listening to what the captain told him. Then he stood smartly to attention in front of the guardhouse door just as he would do if a prisoner had been taken inside!

That thought shook Shakeshaft. What in hell was going on? He sidled up to the sentry.

'Was that Lieutenant Somerville who went inside, Trooper?' he said softly. He offered the man a chaw of tobacco.

The sentry looked at the hard lump of black tobacco, then at Shakeshaft and his lips turned down in an expression of contempt.

'Get lost, 'breed! What goes on here is no

business of you scouts! Stick around and I'll haul you in. Savvy?'

Shakeshaft lifted two fingers at him, spat and wandered away, his mind busy. How to get in contact with Somerville and find out what was in the wind. . . .

But it didn't take long for the rumour to circulate the fort that the lieutenant was to be court-martialled for neglect of duty, causing a situation which might provoke another uprising by the natives, and for mishandling his men. So Somerville was being made the scapegoat because of a few hotheads in his troop who'd gone too far before they were stopped in their tracks by that same officer!

Shakeshaft knew how unfair it was and he was boiling mad. Not one of Somerville's men had come forward to defend him and he, as a civilian scout, had no influence at all.

A week went by, then one day just after noon the great wooden gates of the fort were opened and a contingent of men and wagons rolled through, filling the parade ground.

The members of the court martial panel had arrived and the judging would begin. Shakeshaft waited for the outcome. If it was as he suspected it might be, and Somerville was disgraced and demoted after a jail sentence, then he, Shakeshaft, was going to do something about it.

Moodily he waited for the outcome, sitting

well away from those who were delighting in destroying Somerville's reputation. He didn't even want the company of the other scouts. They eyed him askance and muttered amongst themselves that old Shakeshaft was an ornery bastard.

At last the great doors of the officers' mess hall opened. Shakeshaft studied the faces of the men coming out, and tried to guess the outcome. He threw away his cigarillo, lazily got to his feet and leaned up against one of the bunkhouse veranda uprights. He waited.

Then all became clear. Somerville, looking angry was being escorted to the jailhouse like any common private. So that was it. Somervile was taking the rap for the vile misconduct of his men!

Shakeshaft quietly made his way to the corral where the officers' mounts were kept and made sure that Somerville's horse was tethered near to the wooden gate. All the horse's accoutrements were on a wooden horse close by. It would be quick and easy to saddle up and be gone before the alarm was raised. His own mare was in a corral near the perimeter of the fort. It was only a matter of gathering up food and ammunition for two, making sure the water canteens were full and the bedrolls hidden somewhere close by for a quick getaway.

If Somerville was to be disgraced and demoted, then there was no way that Shakeshaft would scout for any other officer. His loyalty lay with Somerville who'd always treated him as a man and not something little better than an animal.

The cooks were used to his comings and goings and he had the run of the kitchens, for scouts left the fort at odd hours and they could be relied on to take what was necessary for them and leave the cooks to their own business. Now, using the usual procedure, he visited the kitchens late that night and a sleepy cook on call couldn't have cared less about what he was packing away in two duffel bags.

He watched the night hawk in charge of the officers' horses smoke a cigarette and walk up and down awhile until he saw the horses settled for the night. Then the man sat down on a bale of hay and took out a bottle to while the night away in a hazy blur.

When his head drooped and the bottle rolled from his hand, that was the signal for Shakeshaft to make his move. Quietly he unloosed the lieutenant's horse, threw his saddle across his back, and led him away holding on to the bridle firmly so that the horse couldn't shake his head and rattle his harness.

It was all too easy. The fort hadn't been put on alert for a couple of years and the guards had become sloppy.

The biggest problem was getting Somerville

out of jail but he had figured out how to tackle that, too. There was a skylight in the storeroom, where extra rifles and ammuntion were stored. It let light into a murky room that otherwise had no windows for security reasons. It was easy to climb up and break the window gently, catching the shards of glass on a sticky patch of old leather before they fell inwards. Then he slid through the narrow window frame and waited, but there was no alarm. Probably the guard on duty was already asleep, which was all to the good. He eased the door open and saw the faint light from a candle. The guard was sleeping with a rifle across his knees. Beyond him was the cell bars and door. The way was clear.

Shakeshaft saw that the man on duty was a bully of a sergeant who'd treated Shakeshaft badly, so he had no compunction in cold-cocking him as he slept. The man never knew what hit him.

Then swiftly Shakeshaft hunted for the keys of the cells and found them hung up behind a desk.

Somerville, disturbed by the racket, was standing by the cell door, gripping the bars tightly.

'Who is it?'

'It's me, Shakeshaft. I've come to get you.' He fumbled with the keys to find the right one.

'Hell, Shakeshaft, I'll be deserting if I leave now! I've got six months to serve and then I'll be

31

free, but I'll be downgraded to private,' he told the scout bitterly.

'It's your choice, Somerville. I'm not staying to scout for any other bastard who looks down on me! You were different. You see me as I really am, a man in my own right. Now are you coming with me or are you going to let yourself be humiliated?'

Somerville rubbed his bristly chin.

'Come to think of it, the army hasn't shown me any trust. Took those lying bastards' statements so that I took the rap. Go on, open up, Shakeshaft. Better to be hunted and a free man than rotting here in this foul place!'

Shakeshaft gave a reckless laugh and opened up the iron-barred door.

'That's the way I figured it, Somerville. Let's be on our way. Your horse is ready to ride and we can be well on our way before dawn!'

THREE

Geoff Potterson hummed a little tune, one of the bawdy songs he'd learned at medical school on Saturday nights when the students let their hair down in the local tavern, and urged his horses into a faster trot, as they strained to pull the heavily loaded wagon uphill. The tune lifted his spirits, helped to relieve the mighty loneliness that sometimes overcame him in this wild new land.

He thought of the circumstances of why he was here in America at all. He'd never ever expected to be so far away from home and it was all because Ned Hastings had suggested they go and see the old man who ran his macabre business of selling on newly buried bodies to the students and faculty of the Edinburgh School of Medicine.

It wasn't because they'd bought the body; the faculty had turned a blind eye to that, but it was what they'd done with it afterwards. Full of ale, the students had thought it a lark to take it back to the dissecting rooms after midnight and do some experiments not sanctioned by their tutors.

The result had been a hilarious drunken orgy when all the students wanted to show their prowess with the knife and arguments had erupted. The result was that the caretaker had heard the row and called the head and there had been hell to pay. All had been expelled for behaviour unfit for student surgeons and Geoff's father, a doctor, had been appalled and outraged.

'What do you think would happen to my practice,' he'd thundered, 'if this scandal got out? My son, a drunken hooligan! Caught cutting up a body dug up by grave robbers! My God, boy, I can't believe it! There's nothing for you but to emigrate! No other medical school would take you on!'

So that was why Geoff Potterson now found himself the owner of a wagon filled to bursting point with Dr Markham's Elixir of Life, guaranteed to cure the ague, piles, concretion of the bowels, impotence and hangovers along with various women's complaints. He also carried a cream made from pig lard with various noisome substances added, which could be used as a face cream, a cure for boils, scabies and blistered bottoms.

Geoff Potterson reasoned that no matter what

ailed a fellow, he had what it would take to heal him. He also had his own medical kit with him, so he reckoned he'd be welcome wherever he went.

He joined a wagon train travelling west and got his first experiences on the trail, mostly broken bones after fights in saloons or the odd bullet to prise out of flesh. This was something new. He'd never coped with a bullet in Edinburgh. Then, as the wagon train continued west, he felt confident enough to carry on to the next town by himself.

He hummed to keep his spirits up. He'd not seen anyone for hours. It seemed he was alone in this great, wild, most magnificent wilderness.

But suddenly he wasn't alone any more. There were yelling men surrounding him, men he'd never seen the like of before. They were nearly naked and wearing feathers in their black hair. Their copper skins gleamed because of the buffalo grease smeared on them.

The two horses snorted and plunged as he instinctively pulled on the reins in his sudden fear. He could smell himself. His bowels had turned to water.

A yelling brave rode at him. He leaned over, dragged him from the wagon and carried him, helplessly flailing his legs to free himself. All the while the brave, who was a youth younger than himself, shrieked and yelled in triumph.

Then he was dropped to the ground. Before he could shake his head and rise, they were upon him, tearing off his clothes and hooting and laughing at his white skin.

He tried to kick free but they only jeered. One of them built a small fire under a tree, put a stout branch over it and before Geoff understood what they meant to do, he was strung up by his thumbs and hanging over a small smoky fire.

What a way to die, was his last thought as the smoke overcame him. His head hung on his chest as he gave in to the pain in his hands and shoulders.

He was oblivious to the ransacking of his wagon. The youths tossed out all his personal gear and ignored his medical kit. They were looking for whiskey, and they thought they had found it when they found the bottles of Dr Markham's Elixir of Life and the jars of cream.

Laughing and hooting, they plastered cream on their faces and bodies and then opened the bottles and drank, each man sampling several bottles. It was a contest who could drink the most and the empty bottles were flung in a heap by the ransacked wagon.

Then the first howl went up as the first brave clutched his stomach. He scuttled into the undergrowth and soon they were all squatting and raising a stink.

They rolled around in agony between bouts of diarrhoea and gusts of wind, until at last they lay still, faint and exhausted.

The fire died down, unattended and the man they had been going to have fun with was forgotten. He hung from the tree-branch motionless and still as if he was already dead.

Then the leader of the hunting party managed to struggle up on to his jelly-like legs, his belly still cramping.

'It's the white man's magic! He's put a curse on that firewater! The sooner we are away from here the better before he comes back to haunt us!' They heaved themselves upright, mounted up and disappeared again into the undergrowth. Once again all was still.

Far away to the east, Shakeshaft and Somerville saw the dust cloud. They pulled up their horses and climbed a ridge to see better. Both knew that the army would now be looking for them and Shakeshaft also knew that he wouldn't be very popular if he ran into a band of Indians. So it was with interest they watched the Indians riding away, not at their usual headlong gallop but at more of a trot. Some of them were hanging over their pony's necks.

'Seems like that band of Cheyenne is in trouble,' mused Shakeshaft, 'but there was no gunfire. Most peculiar.'

'Maybe we should take a look; follow their trail back over and see what happened.'

'A good idea. We've nothing better to do.'

So slowly and carefully they retraced the Indians tracks and came upon the naked man hanging by his thumbs over a slow fire.

'Holy Mother! What in hell is a lone man doing out here in Indian territory?'

'And why should those heathens leave him in such a hurry?'

Intrigued, they cautiously inched their horses forward until they were only a few yards from the hanging man. They noted his white soft-muscled body, the hanging head of curly brown hair and, more important, the smouldering embers of the fire, which were sending up wisps of smoke as if the man was being kippered.

'It looks like something happened to spook those Indians,' Somerville guessed and spat on the ground. 'I reckon the feller, whoever he is, is dead as last week's beef.'

Shakeshaft cocked his head in the direction of the wagon and its strewed contents.

'Maybe we should take a look-see at what the feller was freighting. There's a whole heap of bottles over there. He must be some kind of city quack.

They dismounted and started to make their way over to the wagon when a groan stopped them in their tracks.

'Holy Mother of God!' Somerville spluttered, 'the lucky bastard's still alive!' They ran across to the suspended body and sure enough there was some twitching of the legs. Swiftly, Shakeshaft cut the rawhide bonds while Somerville held onto the inert body and took the weight of the helpless man so that he didn't fall into the embers of the fire.

They laid him down in the dirt, stared into the bearded face and waited for the eyelids to open.

'You reckon he's dying?' Somerville asked. Shakeshaft shook his head.

'There's no wounds. Those Cheyenne braves were going to have some fun with him but something spooked them. I wonder what it was?'

Somerville didn't answer but walked over to the pile of bottles. He also noticed there were empty jars along with the bottles. He picked up one bottle and smelled it. His nose wrinkled. He coughed.

'I don't know what's been in these bottles but whatever it was is mighty putrid!

'It's the Elixir of Life,' a hoarse voice proclaimed faintly, as Somerville came back carrying a bottle.

Both men looked at the stranger who was now shivering.

'Hell! We'd better get him a blanket or something. I don't see his clothes lying around.'

'The wagon.' The faint voice was becoming a

little stronger. 'If those goddamn heathens haven't fired the wagon, there should be extra clothes in there.'

It took a while to get the fellow clothed for every movement of his arms and shoulders was excruciating. A good shot of rotgut whiskey helped.

They propped him up under the tree he'd swung from.

'Now just tell us why you were travelling alone in this territory? Didn't you know it was dangerous?'

'I was with a wagon train but they were going west and I wanted to make my way south, so we parted. I was told a cowtown was only a few hours away. I must have taken a wrong turning.'

'I take it you're a quack. Am I right?' asked Somerville.

'Sort of. I'm a doctor from Scotland.' At their look of surprise, he went on: 'I've been in America for around three months.' He looked from one to the other. He wasn't going to tell them he was only a student and had not passed his finals. It didn't matter a hoot what he'd done back home.

'So that's why the peculiar accent. I was trying to guess where you came from.' Somerville laughed. 'What's your name, feller?'

'Potterson ... er ... Geoff Potterson, Doctor Potterson to be exact.'

40

'Right! We'll call you Doc. I'm Abe Somerville and this is Shakeshaft.'

'Shakeshaft? That's a hell of a name!' Doc tried to laugh but it hurt.

Shakeshaft stiffened for a moment. Was this feller going to be like all the rest of white men? Then he relaxed, as Doc said hoarsely:

'I've got to thank you men for saving my life. I'll not forget it.'

'What about having a swig out of one of your own bottles?'

Doc gave a broken laugh.

'Is there any left? Those red devils were drinking as if they were bottles of booze! No wonder they went off as they did! Their bowels would turn to water! I don't reckon to drink the stuff. I only sell it!'

The two men looked at each other and Shakeshaft's face split into a grin.

'So the Cheyenne can never say their bowels never turn to water because of the White-eyes! Those young braves will never live it down! They are a disgrace to their people!'

The two men laughed, much to the puzzlement of Doc Potterson, who was massaging his shoulders.

'Why a disgrace?'

'Because the young fools didn't know the difference between white man's firewater and that stuff you're toting!'

41

Geoff Potterson looked a little bemused.

'Maybe I shouldn't ask, but does it matter? I don't understand.'

The two men looked at him in amazement and then at each other, and Somerville said unbelievingly,

'Don't you know anything about the Indians? Didn't the wagon master wise you up on this country?'

Geoff Potterson shook his head.

'Never saw much of him. He was riding ahead and I was sort of lagging behind the train. I did get friendly with a family but they cut off before I did. I guess everyone thought I was an experienced traveller.'

Shakeshaft eyed him grimly.

'I reckon you're a lamb waiting to be slaughtered. I guess you'd better travel along with us. Mind you, it could be dangerous.' He looked at Somerville and laughed. 'You could describe us as wanted men ... both by the army and the Cheyenne!'

Geoff Potterson stared from one to the other, a little horrified.

'You're not outlaws, are you? My God, I've jumped from the frying-pan into the fire!'

'Not outlaws,' Somerville said easily. 'I'm a deserter and he helped me to escape, and he's wanted by the Cheyenne for just being himself! If you tag along with us, you've got to be prepared for anything. Have you got a gun and can you use it?'

Geoff Potterson licked his lips.

'I've got a shotgun I bought from an old man in New York but I've never fired it. I've got ammunition for it though . . .' he added in a rush as he saw the look of disgust pass between this strange pair.

Somerville shook his head.

'You're lucky to be alive, mister, in more ways than one. I think when those shoulders heal, we'll be giving you some lessons on gunplay. What d'you think, Shakeshaft?'

'I guess he's no good to us otherwise. How are you on a horse, Doc?' Potterson shrugged helplessly.

'Never been on a horse in my life. That's why I bought the wagon and the horses. I can manage them.'

'Thank God, you're good at something!' Then a thought struck Shakeshaft. 'Can you dig a slug out of a feller's arm?'

Geoff Potterson flushed. 'I'm not skilled at digging out bullets, but I managed to take out several on the trail.' He looked at both men, 'I'm sorry, there was no call for extracting bullets back in Scotland, but I can cut a body open and take out an appendix . . .' He saw the two men looking at him blankly.

'Hell's teeth!' growled Somerville. 'It seems

you're going to be nothing but dead weight! We should never have come to see what those Cheyenne were up to!'

'Oh, I don't know . . . he's a big feller and he's alive. With any luck we can make him over. Give him a chance, Abe.'

Geoff Potterson listened. They were talking about him as if he wasn't there. They weren't impressed with him, which was something new for Potterson. As far as they were concerned, he was nothing but a nuisance and a liability. He watched them walk away and talk to each other in low tones for a few minutes. When they returned to him he was relieved to hear Shakeshaft say in solemn tones:

'We're not dumping you, Doc. We reckon you need educating and if you tag along with us, we'll teach you all you should know.'

'Teach me!' he spluttered, thinking of his expensive education. 'I don't think you're in a position to teach me anything!'

'No? Then how come you rode into a band of Indians like a blind fool, or why did you risk travelling alone, eh?'

'But there was no other way to go and I was the only one going to Copper's Creek, and as for those demons, they just rose up out of the ground!'

'That wagon master should be shot!' Somerville said grimly, 'The goddamn low-down swine knew the danger you would be in. Did you hand over any cash before the trail began?'

'Yes, he asked for two hundred dollars. He said he had expenses of the journey to meet.' Somerville glanced at Shakeshaft and nodded.

'I bet my last dollar that was Jeb Williams. The son of a bitch has done it before. 'He turned to Geoff Potterson. 'Lesson number one, mister, never give over cash before the job's done! Number two is don't take folk on face value. There could be another face behind the mask!'

Geoff swallowed. These men might look rough. Back home he would have looked on these smelly, bearded men with haughty distaste and lectured them about cleanliness and all he knew about bugs.

'Thank you. I'll remember that,' he managed to utter.

Geoff, still recovering from his ordeal, lay on the hard ground and watched fascinated while the two men built a small fire around some flat stones. In no time at all they had a blackened coffee pot standing on a smooth stone and surrounded by flames. He could smell coffee bubbling away. Then he watched Shakeshaft make flat pancakes in a battered frying pan with flour and water and a little of their precious salt, and Geoff reckoned that these two men could teach him something after all. He'd never cooked anything in his, what he would now think of nostalgically, pampered life.

He ate his pancake with gusto along with a thick slice of pickled pork which had once been part of army rations. He felt better after he'd eaten. The shock of his ordeal was now dissipating. He managed to stagger to his feet to go and rummage in his medicine bag. He came back to the fire with a small brown bottle of laudanum.

The two men watched with interest.

'What in hell's that?' asked Somerville.

'Laudanum. Good for sleeping. I thought I'd take a small dose for my aches and pains.'

'Like hell you will!' Somerville snatched it from him and was about to throw it away when Geoff grabbed for it.

'Hey! Don't do that! It's precious, and what business is it of yours if I take it?' The two men glared at each other, while Shakeshaft lounged close by, picking his teeth with a small sliver of wood.

'Because no man in his right mind would knock himself out in these parts! You've got to be aware that hostiles, and not only Indians, might creep up on you at all times! Even at night, you sleep with one eye open. Savvy?'

Geoff looked around nervously.

'Everything seems quiet,' he said sulkily. 'I didn't think—'

'That's your trouble, mister, you don't think!

Now you bed down over there with your feet towards the fire.'

'I could sleep in the wagon. I've got a bed in there . . .'

'Look, feller, do as I say. The first you know of an Indian raid could be a burning arrow in the tarpaulin of the wagon. If you're inside, then you can kiss your chances goodbye!'

'Oh!'

'So be sensible and just do as me and my pard say. Me and him will share the watch over night. From tomorrow we expect you to share watches with us. Right?'

'Right. '

At dawn, Geoff was roughly shaken awake. He opened bleary eyes. Hell! He'd only had a few hours of restless sleep and when he *had* slept he'd dreamed of red devils stringing him up. He yawned lazily.

'Rise and shine, Doc, if you want to eat before we move on,' Shakeshaft said sharply. He was already dousing the small fire and scattering the embers and Geoff reached for the coffeepot. Evidently they had eaten earlier.

'I must have a wash and shave . . .' he began.

'You can cut out any ideas like that, Doc. Where we're going you'll be lucky to get a dunk in the river now and again!'

Geoff ate a scrappy meal of last night's leavings of pancakes. They didn't taste so good this morning. His belly still rumbled when at last they were ready to ride.

He viewed the mound of empty bottles and jars with anger. Those sons of bitches had ruined any profit he might have made on this first journey west. Then he roughly put the rest of his gear in some kind of order and when the two men rode out of camp, he followed behind, awkwardly handling the reins of his horses because of his pulled muscles.

The trail they were following petered out to scrubland; the wagon bounced alarmingly and Geoff gritted his teeth. These fellers were mad to try and cross country like this! He would never in a million years have attempted a hair-raising trek like this!

His backside ached and his ribs felt as if they'd crack under the jarring of the wagon bed. It was agony but he was determined to hide his suffering.

Shakeshaft rode back once to ask him if he was OK.

'Yes, no problem,' he'd answered briefly, 'but why travel over this god-forsaken land? Why not stick to the proper trail?'

Shakeshaft looked at him half in amusement and half in amazed puzzlement.

'You know, Doc, I've never met anyone like you before. You're as ignorant as a new-born babe! Let's spell it out one more time. I'm wanted by the Cheyenne, and Somerville is wanted by the army for desertion. You come with us and you're in the same danger we are. The only way we can get out of this territory is to dodge our pursuers. Oh, yes,' at Geoff's look of surprise. 'Just because we don't actually see anyone after us, doesn't mean that no one is following behind! We're playing a cat and mouse game. If you've taken note, we're travelling over hard stony ground and your wagon is helping to blot out our tracks. Why do you think we insisted you hung those branches at the back of the wagon?'

'I don't know and I didn't like to ask. I assumed they were for fires if we camped where there was no brushwood.'

Shakeshaft laughed.

'We don't rely on wood for our fires. We use dung or do without! We're gonna cross desert land with a scarcity of water and you've got to learn to know where to look for it, if it's to be found.' He looked at the listening Somerville, his mouth twisting wryly. 'You might even have to drink your own piss!'

Geoff Potter's look of shocked disgust made Somerville laugh.

'Only in emergencies, Doc, When you're up against a rock and a hard place, even your own piss is welcome!'

'That's the worst case, Doc. But we're gonna

49

teach you to look for cactus plants that hold
water and roots that the Cheyenne use as both
food and water. The desert abounds with food
from snakes and muskrats and even fat grubs.
It's only a matter of knowing where to look!'

'I see I've a whole lot to learn,' Geoff said
humbly. 'I reckon all I learned at school means
nothing here.'

'Too right, Doc. This is a whole new world for
you and you've got to think of us as your life-
lines!'

They rode until dark. Shakeshaft and
Somerville took turns to ride ahead, climb on to
a promontory and scan the scene around them
for dust clouds or signs of Indians trailing them.

All seemed quiet, but Geoff saw that the two
men were alert and vigilant at all times. Even
birds, disturbed by their passing, brought an
instant reflex as hands went to guns.

Geoff sweated and strained at the reins of the
horses. His shoulders ached, not only from his
ordeal at the hands of the Indians but also from
gripping the reins tightly all day. He hadn't got
the knack of letting the horses pick the easiest
path for themselves. He saw every bump in the
ground as a potential hazard.

It was a relief when Somerville called a halt
near a shallow river. Immediately he was ready to
unload his camping gear but Shakeshaft came to
him with arms akimbo.

'And what the hell do you think you're doing?'

Geoff looked up in surprise.

'Getting the camping gear out. What else?'

'You don't need all that stuff. No bedroll for us tonight. We bunk down on the ground, our saddles as pillows and one blanket to cover us. We use the bedrolls when we're safe, not before. We'll all take turns tonight to watch. Me first, you second and Somerville last so that he can wake you if you drop off.'

'But all's quiet . . .'

'Yeah, yeah, yeah . . . that's what you think. All greenhorns think Indians only attack an hour before dawn! Make no mistake, I know they'll attack when they're good and ready. In our case, they'll creep up like shadows and if you're lucky, you'll never know anything about it!'

Geoff swallowed and looked uneasily around at the gently flowing river, the clusters of pine trees, the sparse scrubland dotted with boulders. He wished to hell he'd never come on this trip in the first place. He cursed that stupid fool back in Edinburgh for suggesting cutting up a cadaver.

Shakeshaft showed Geoff how to make a small fire inside a ring of stones so that the fire didn't spread into the trees and dry grass. He used dung and dead wood, explaining that green wood gave off too much black smoke. He

51

noticed their smoke was thin and a wispy grey and that it soon dispersed. He was desperately sick of pickled pork and panbread but he was too hungry to protest that he had extra tins of peaches and beans in the wagon.

For a while the three men talked as they drank coffee. Geoff told them of the circumstances of his coming to America and they listened with interest.

Then Shakeshaft told him of his not being wanted either by the white people or the Cheyenne and of the death of his wife and son. Geoff wanted to know why the Cheyenne were still after him.

'Because I shamed one of their women by taking her as wife. She was killed because she was the wife of a man with tainted blood and my son was killed because he had a tainted father.'

'I'm sorry. To me, you're just another person like myself. I've never come upon racial hatred before.'

'Well, you'll run into plenty of it if you live long enough, I can tell you!' Shakeshaft sounded bitter. He looked at Somerville and smiled. 'The lieutenant here was the only man who treated me like a man in that fort.' he said quietly, 'and that is why I stuck my neck out and got him out of the jailhouse when he was court-martialled. It wasn't his fault his platoon went mad and massacred a village of women and kids and old men.'

Geoff was horrified. 'Oh, God, what a world we're living in!'

Somerville emptied the dregs out of his cup and spat into the fire.

'You'll find all people, whether white or red, are proud and have their own prejudices and beliefs,' he said softly. 'Out here in the wilderness a man's actions are primitive.' He looked from one to the other. Then sighed and said abruptly:

'You know, there was no one with more prejudices than my father. You've both bared your souls. I might as well bare mine!' He stopped and brooded for awhile, staring into the small fire, while the other two waited. Then he went on: 'My father was a hellfire preacher. He preached death and damnation to all sinners on Sundays and during the week he toiled and sweated on a small dirt farm back in Illinois. I was the eldest of nine kids and I watched my ma work herself to death, having kids and working on the land, along with us kids. We worked as soon as we could pull weeds and carry pig pails. She buried three of us and Pa said a brief prayer over them and that was it. If we answered back or smiled at the wrong time he whipped us. He took great pleasure in whipping out the devil in us. I came to hate him.

'Ma died and when my next two brothers were old enough to protect our three sisters from him

I left home. I couldn't stand it any longer. I was green, barely nineteen, and I knew I would never go back home. I became a tumbleweed . . . you might say I was a hobo, a tramp,' he explained at Geoff's look of enquiry, 'then the war came and I joined up and that became my life. So you see, I know what it's like to be an underdog.'

He looked at them both. 'I found that I judged a man by his courage and loyalty, not by who he is. I mixed with white men who were more cruel that any Indians, and I had dealings with many Indians of different tribes who could be both cruel and humane, so you see there is not much difference between people.'

Geoff looked from one to the other, then he stretched out his hands to both and they made an unbroken ring as Geoff said quietly:

'I'm honoured, gentlemen, that you have both become my mentors and protectors. I hope someday to repay you both!'

The two men laughed. It sounded so far-fetched that their greenhorn might do anything for them!

A rough punch on the shoulder brought Geoff awake from an uneasy sleep. It was his turn to take the midnight watch. He stretched and sat up abruptly, aching in every limb. He looked up at Shakeshaft grinning down at him.

'Rise and shine, mister! All's quiet but you

keep your eyes skinned! Now like I said before, keep the fire burning low, and watch the horizon for spooks! It's the Cheyenne you're looking out for. The army boys come during the day, but those hellfire varmints come without warning, so watch your back!'

He grinned again at Geoff's look of near terror.

'OK, Doc, maybe I was exaggerating a little. We're in a good position here and I'd say safe enough until morning but we can't take chances. So just watch it while I get a little shut-eye.' With that, Shakeshaft curled up in a ball near the fire, pulled his hat over his eyes and gave Geoff one last instruction. 'When you see the moon come up between those trees yonder, that's the time to wake up the boss. Give him a kick if he don't wake up straight away. He's a mighty sound sleeper.' Then he seemed to be asleep in an instant.

For a while Geoff watched the two sleeping men. He knew Shakeshaft would be sleeping with one ear cocked like a wild animal. One yell from him and they would be there, guns at the ready. He noticed that both men slept with their weapons close to their hands.

Uneasily he looked about him in the darkness. His nerves were jumping. He could hear small scurryings of nocturnal animals. In the distance a coyote called. He put more wood on the fire and watched the flames leap up. He sat crouched by it warming his hands. He saw that they trembled. Hell! He wasn't cut out for this kind of life!

He heard an owl hoot. Was it an owl, he thought with sick dismay. He'd heard from the men on the wagon train of Indians using owl calls as signals. He got up, walked around the camp and took time to urinate in the under-growth. His eyes ached from peering into the shadows. When a tree branch stirred in the slight breeze he was jumpy.

The half-moon came up, which was no help. It cast light and shadow and conjured up figures that weren't there. Time seemed to stand still.

At last, cold and aching, he went back to the fire, which had now died down again and crouched near it; even its heat seemed to be gone. This first night's watch was one he would never forget.

He watched the moon and prayed silently for it to move more quickly and come up between the trees.

Gradually, as the night wore on, he became calmer, remembering Shakeshaft's words, that it would be a quiet night with no attack. It comforted him and he sat and thought about his life back in Edinburgh and the carefree student days. How stupid he had been to go on that drunken bender which had resulted in him sitting here watching out for scalphunters!

He found himself getting drowsy, his eyes drooped and he had to shake himself to clear his mind. He decided to go down to the stream and dowse his face and head in the water. That would clear all sleep from him.

He moved quietly. He didn't want either man waking up and taking a shot at him. Down at the stream he watched the play of the moonlight on the water. A pretty sight if it hadn't been so damned dangerous. He crouched down and was bending forward to scoop up the water when there came a strange whistling sound and he was just in time to see the glint of a knife as it passed over his head. His heart pounded as he turned sharply. That knife would have buried itself between his shoulder blades if he hadn't been crouching down by the water.

He was just in time to glimpse a figure launching himself on him. He fell backwards into the stream as the Indian grappled with him, his hands seeking his throat.

Geoff wanted to scream and breathe at the same time but instinctively lashed out at the writhing figure on top of him. The Indian's arm was about his neck, holding him under the fast-flowing water. He spluttered and then took a bite at the bulging muscles. He heard the man scream and he tasted blood.

The Indian rolled away in the water; then

both men got to their feet. This time Geoff was ready for him. He hadn't been boxing champion in his undergraduate years for nothing. He caught the Indian on the jaw with a punch that crunched bone.

The Indian screamed again, and staggered backwards. Geoff, suddenly overcome with fury, lunged after him and followed up with several blows to the head and chest.

The Indian's black eyes spat murderous anger as he tried to get in close. He had never wrestled a man who used his fists in that strange manner.

Then with a yell of defiance, the Cheyenne brave kicked Geoff in the groin and turned to flee. It was then, when Geoff was rolling about in agony, that he became aware of the two men watching the fight. He was only half-aware when a gunshot rang out and Geoff saw the smoking pistol in Somerville's hand.

Shakeshaft came and helped him to his feet.

'You all right?'

'Yes, I suppose so. I feel as if I've been gelded.'

Shakeshaft laughed.

'You're lucky he didn't have a second knife or you might have been!'

'What happened? Did he get away?'

'Nope! The boss got him in the back.'

Geoff looked to where Somerville was crouched over the dead body. Only now did the reality of it all sink in. He'd fought his first Indian!

Then Somerville walked over to them both.

'I think we'd better break camp and be on our way. That feller was a scout and they'll be out hunting for him by dawn. You did well, Doc. I didn't think you'd have the guts. Where did you learn to fight like that?'

Geoff managed a grin.

'Back home in Edinburgh. We weren't cutting up bodies all the time. We did have our moments. Boxing was one way to impress the girls!'

'Ah!' Somerville laughed. 'Spoken like a true man! I think we'll make a frontiersman of you yet!'

FOUR

After two more days of trekking Geoff was mightily sick of the rolling, bumping wagon. It was as if the two men chose routes that should never have been travelled by a lumbering wagon.

It wasn't as if there was much of a load now that most of his bottles and jars had been pilfered by those damned raiders, fumed Geoff to himself. Most of his personal stuff he could do without, now that he knew what it was like to live rough.

His companions didn't worry about clean underwear or extra shirts. When the opportunity arose, they plunged into a stream, rubbed themselves with some foul weed called soapwort, which lathered up like real soap, and then dowsed their stinking clothes and rubbed them on stones, like the natives did, and put them out to dry in the sun. God knows what they did in winter when the snows came. Geoff guessed they didn't bother at all.

He saw Abe Somerville looking questioningly at the wagon.

'Something the matter, Abe?'

'Yeah, I've been thinking. It's time to get rid of that there wagon. It looks like it's served its purpose and we got the army foxed, so now we should get you a horse and then we can move faster and go over some rough country.'

'Rough country? I thought we were already doing that!'

Somerville smiled.

'Mister, you ain't seen anything yet! You've had it easy. Wait until we get down nearer to Mexico. We'll come to some real mountainous stuff.'

'Is that where we're heading? Mexico?'

'Yes, with luck. We'll cross the Rio Grande and once over the border the army can kiss us good-bye! You object to that?'

Geoff shook his head.

'It doesn't matter to me where I go. I'd rather ride with you to hell than be on my own in this damned country!' He looked around uneasily.

'You can relax, Doc. Shakeshaft was away last night, scouting around and there's no sign of the varmints hunting for him. I reckon that scout you tangled with was out on his own and so the wagon was never reported back to the Cheyenne. They'll miss him and trace his tracks in time, but we'll be long gone by then.'

61

Geoff shuddered, remembering his fear when he was strung up by his thumbs. . . .

'So what do we do about the wagon?'

'We'll trade it for a horse when we come to the first settlement. Wagons are in short supply. We'll get a good trade. You leave the dickering with us.'

'But I can't ride! I've never been on a horse before!'

'Jesus Christ! What else don't you know? You've been badly brought up, Doc!'

'I'm sorry,' Geoff said humbly. 'Coming to America was the last thing on my folks' mind when I was growing up. I had my head stuck in books. Father said I was to be a doctor from the day I was born. I had no choice.'

'So why pack you off to America after a drunken lark got out of hand? All students do mad things some time in their lives.'

'I'm afraid pride meant more to him than I did,' Geoff answered mournfully. Then he brightened up. 'If I'd stayed I would never have heard the last of it. Out here I'm my own man!'

'Well said, Doc! This here land makes or breaks a man. I sure want to see you make it! There's not many sawbones around these parts.'

'Look, I'm not a qualified doctor. I didn't pass my finals,' Geoff answered apologetically. 'but I know a lot in theory. It's just that I never had the opportunity to practise.'

'No matter,' Somerville answered cheerfully. 'I reckon half the docs during the war learnt their trade the hard way! As long as you can combat lead poisoning and fever, you'll do!'

Geoff sighed. There was a lot more to medicine than that.

The trail had become monotonous and Geoff was beginning to think that the danger from the Cheyenne and the army was over. They must be well out of their territory now. When he'd asked where they were, Somerville had laughed and said they were not too far from the Rio Grande, which meant nothing to Geoff. He was now more used to the jolting of the wagon but each night he was glad to get down and stretch himself before bedding down on the hard ground.

Shakeshaft now told him that this was Mescallero Indian country and the Cheyenne were left behind. He seemed easier now but warned Geoff that the Mescalleros could be mighty dangerous at times.

'You've met up with them before?'

Shakeshaft nodded. 'Yeah. Years ago when I lived with the Cheyenne. I was with them on a hunting trip. We found ourselves in Mescallero territory and it was a running battle to get back into our own land. Sly, pesky devils, they are, so we'll have to watch out carefully.'

From then on, Geoff watched uneasily as they

slowly travelled on and when at last they came to a small settlement, he sighed with relief.

The cluster of buildings straggled along a narrow main street. There were small white adobe houses, a church and a couple of saloons, one of which had an extended stable for travellers' horses. There was a store which seemed to sell everything including guns and ammunition. There was a faded sign on a post which indicated that this was Digger's Gulch with the number of inhabitants originally as 309 with the 9 crossed out to 8 and then on down to 294.

Geoff reckoned it wasn't a very healthy place to live.

He drew up in front of the bigger saloon when he saw the two men dismount and tie their horses to the hitching rail. He followed them inside. It was dim and smelled of stale ale and the fusty odour of mould. The floor was of packed earth, the bar was a couple of planks supported on two wooden barrels which had splintered holes in them. To a goggle-eyed Geoff, they looked like bullet holes.

'Three beers, pronto,' barked Somerville, and the fat barman in the dirty apron jumped to it. He recognized the signs of authority at once. He also noticed the low-slung army pistol tied to the stranger's leg.

They all drank appreciatively. When they were

on their second drink, Somerville asked to speak to the boss.

'What you want him for?' the barman asked surlily. 'He don't usually talk to strangers.'

'Mind your own business! Just get him!'

Sulkily, the barman wiped his hands on his apron and slouched away into a back room. Then he returned and stood at the door. He said nothing but pointed with his thumb behind him. Somerville nodded and he and Shakeshaft entered the back room after Shakeshaft had said quietly to Geoff:

'Doc, you stay here and watch that bastard while we do the dickering. Right?'

Geoff nodded. He had time to look about him now, his eyes having become accustomed to the gloom.

He saw several rickety tables and benches; one bench was now occupied by an old man with a bald head and white beard. He seemed to be nodding over his beer. Two men in a corner were talking in whispers and glancing occasionally at Geoff. They were small men, swarthy, Mexican most likely. Geoff remembered that the Mexicans' first weapon was the knife. He wished he was proficient with both the knife and the gun. He would suggest a few lessons from his two new friends when they got out of here.

The old man snorted and looked up. Geoff saw that he wore a black eye-patch. The man drank the rest of his beer down, then heaved himself upright and lurched to the bar.

'Another beer, Juan.'

'Don't you think you've had enough, Sam?'

'Never enough, Juan. Just gimme another.' Juan obliged.

The old man scratched his head and looked at Geoff.

'You a stranger in these parts? I haven't seen you around.'

'Just passing through.' Geoff took a gulp of beer.

'Can you spare a few cents for an old man, mister? I'm an old soldier, wounded in the cause of freedom!'

The barman grinned. 'Take no notice of the old fool! He was in no war, he lost his eye in a fight over a woman!'

'You mind your own goddamn business, Juan! You have no call to tell lies about me!'

'Lies? You son of a bitch! Everyone knows about that fight you had with Rodriguez, all those years ago! He cut out your eye and you sliced his throat open and he bled to death on this here floor. There's the stain over there to prove it, and you didn't get Maria after all the goddamn fighting! She went off with that Americano who promised her silken sheets! I know. I was there as a kid and I saw it all!'

'If you'd kept your big mouth shut, I might

have paid you something off the slate!'

'Like hell you would! You'd have gone next door and spent this greenhorn's cash on Eduardo's rotgut pulque!'

Sam turned away mumbling something about big mouthed bastards and then turned again to Geoff, his one eye gleaming wickedly.

'You want to see the hole in my face? It's a rare sight!'

Geoff, taken aback, nodded.

'It'll cost you. '

Intrigued, Geoff dug into his pocket and pulled out a dime.

'Will this do?' A claw hand clutched it. It went into a pocket, then the black patch was whipped off and Sam displayed his eye-socket proudly.

'There you are! Does that turn your stomach? I've seen strong men puke at the sight of it!'

'No,' said Geoff cooly. 'I've seen worse sights than that.' He eyed the puckered scar tissue.

'Oh? And what sights may they have been, eh? Or are you just boasting, mister? You don't look old enough to have seen many gory sights!'

'I've seen bodies slit open. I've handled livers and hearts and measured intestines. I've seen a brain taken from a skull . . .'

Sam stopped him. He was looking pale under the dirt ingrained in his skin.

'You're kidding! What kind of devils would do things like that? What tribe of Indians were they?'

67

Geoff smiled.

'No Indians, Sam. It all happened back home in Scotland!'

'Holy Mother of God! Those there Scots must be more uncivilized than the natives in these parts! I never heard of them doing things like cutting brains out of skulls! They roast folk alive and use prisoners for target practice, but never that!'

'I'm a doctor. It was all done in the name of science.'

'A doctor, eh?' Sam looked Geoff up and down as if he was a new specimen of manhood.

'We don't get many around here. My eye now, it was bound up and it healed itself. When I felt a squirmy tickle behind the eyepatch I cleaned it out. It was usually after a fly had laid eggs and they'd hatched. The grubs ate any putrid flesh and eventually the socket healed. I didn't need no so-called doctor.'

'You were lucky.'

'Yeah, I suppose so.' The old man stood brooding for a while, then said abruptly: 'You got anything for piles?'

Geoff thought of the few jars of ointment he had left from the Indian raid. The jars had supposedly been for the ladies, to soften weathered skin, but what the hell . . .

'What about a jar of ointment? I've some jars on the wagon that are guaranteed to cure blisters, heat rashes, piles and sore gums. I'll give you a jar.'

Sam handed back his dime.

'Yeah, I'd appreciate that. You're a good guy, Doc!'

Out of the corner of his eye, Geoff saw the door of the back room open. A young girl slipped through and hurried out of the saloon. A few minutes later she returned followed by a tall, cadaverous man who looked about sixty. His face was ravaged with pain.

Geoff wondered who he and the girl were and was curious. Was it to do with Somerville and Shakeshaft's visit with the owner of the saloon?

Sam nudged Geoff.

'That's the boss's daughter. A rare comely lass. I noticed you took a good gander at her!' He chuckled. 'The boss will shoot any feller who dares touch her! She's special.'

'And who was the fellow with her?'

'That's the boss's brother. He runs the store.' Now all was clear to Geoff. He waited eagerly for the men to return.

'What about my pile ointment?'

'You'll get it, old man, when we go to unload the wagon.'

'You got other stuff to sell? Purgatives and the like?'

'Sort of,' answered Geoff, thinking of the few bottles that had escaped the carnage.

69

'We could do with some medical supplies around here.'

Just then the door opened and a smiling Somerville, puffing on a cigar, came out with Shakeshaft close behind. He winked at Geoff and gave a little nod.

Then followed the tall thin man and a giant of a man with grizzled whiskers and a beer belly. So this was the boss.

'This is Doctor Potterson,' Somerville said formally to the two men, waving at Geoff, 'and these two gentlemen are Isaac Sloane and Mordecai Sloane. We've traded your horses and wagon and some of the contents for a riding-horse, a pack-horse, some staples and an army pistol and ammo.'

'And if you'll look at my arm, Doc,' the thin man broke in, 'I'll toss in a Spencer Repeater rifle, as good as new and enough ammo to fight an army!'

Geoff looked at Somerville, who was looking anxious but he nodded as if to encourage Geoff and his look stopped Geoff from blurting out that he was only a student. He gulped.

'Yes, of course. What's the matter with your arm?'

'Got blasted a few weeks ago. Lost my left hand and the stump's not healed right.' Eagerly he took off his apron and stripped off his dirty flannel shirt, exposing a thin wasted body. Geoff was shocked at what he saw.

The man thrust out an arm covered in bloody bandages. He began unwinding them and the stench began to permeate the air. Geoff strove to control a coughing fit.

He recognized that stench. It was a smell one never forgot. The man's stump was gangrenous.

He stared at the black blood and encrusted pus and the tell-tale blue-red signs creeping up his arm. Jesus Christ! What was he to do with that?

'I want you to cut my arm off by the elbow,' the quiet voice was saying. 'You as a doc can do this?'

Geoff nodded. He was having trouble speaking, but without a word, he went outside to the wagon. He brought back his medical kit and also a jar of ointment for Sam. His hands were shaking but he knew the man would be dead within weeks if nothing drastic was done.

'I'll have to have more light and we'll have to scrub the bar top down before we can start. '

Isaac Sloane yelled at the watching men.

'All right, you gawpers! Get out. And you too, Sam. We don't want your bad breaths polluting the place!' The three men slunk out.

'I should really scrub up and wear proper overalls but I have none.'

'Don't mess about, just get on with the job,' roared Isaac. 'I want my brother fit and well again and if you can do it, then there's nothing

I wouldn't do for you!'

So Geoff closed his eyes and prayed while Mordecai clambered on to the bar top and laid himself down ready for what had to be done.

Somerville and Shakeshaft watched interestedly. This was the first time they'd seen their new friend in action.

Geoff opened his case and selected the saw and the scalpels he might need and turned to Shakeshaft.

'Keep that fire burning bright. I'll have to cauterize the wound afterwards.'

Suddenly he felt confident. The moment he'd handled his familiar tools a strange calmness had come over him. He was in charge. Somehow he knew the proceedings would go well.

He reached for the bottle of chloroform and shook out a measure on to one of his own bandages. He watched Mordecai relax and go to sleep; then he got on with the job . . . .

The cauterizing and bandaging were over when Mordecai awakened.

'When are you going to start?' he asked drowsily.

Geof smiled down at him.

'It's over, Mordecai. All you have to do now is keep that stump clean. Your niece can change the bandages for you.'

Mordecai nodded groggily and lay back on the bar counter. 'Never felt like this since I got kicked by a mule,' he complained.

'Take it easy for a few days. Let others look after the store and you'll be fine.'

'I owe you the rifle and ammo. Isaac will get them for you.'

'Thank you.'

Suddenly Geoff was overcome with reaction and the smell of the fetid saloon. He had to get out. Beads of sweat ran down his face.

'I want some fresh air,' he gasped. He stumbled out of the saloon and was faced with a small crowd of men, women and children. He looked at them with amazement.

Old Sam stepped out from behind a bunch of women, his nearly toothless mouth split wide open.

'Doc, I told them what you were doing for Mordecai and these good folk want you to help them too!'

Geoff was taken aback. His eyes wandered over a thin pale-faced woman with an arm around a boy of about twelve years of age, and then at a couple of men, who obviously had been in a fight. There were others, all looking hopeful.

'Doc? You're here to help them, aren't you?' Sam's voice had pleading in it. Geoff cleared his throat.

'I'll do what I can. Maybe you should all come into the saloon.' Then he turned to the woman

73

and young boy. 'What seems to be the trouble, ma'am?'

'He's got a huge boil on his neck and he's been breaking out in boils since last winter. This one's very bad.'

Geoff saw that the inflamed skin around the boil was about to burst.

'Hmm, I'll have to lance it, ma'am.' He looked down kindly at the frightened child. 'Don't be frightened, boy, it'll be all over in a flash and you'll feel much better. What's your name?'

'Benjy, sir.'

'Well, Benjy, come inside and we'll soon have you better.'

Geoff's first panic had dissipated as soon as he got to work. There seemed to be a never-ending stream of folk with all kinds of ailments, some easily remedied and others more complicated, but all looked up to him with respect. He was elated in spirit, but physically he was exhausted.

After the last patient had gone he sighed and sat down at one of the tables.

'I could use a drink!' The barman hurried to him with a bottle and glass.

'Drink all you want, sir. The boss says you got the freedom of the house and supper's coming up pronto!'

He was on his second glass of whiskey when Somerville and Shakeshaft came in. They had been disposing of the wagon and finishing off trading. They grinned at him.

'You sure made a hit with these folk, Doc! Isaac's made arrangements for you tonight. We, on the other hand, have to bed down here . . . free of course, but you're in for the night of your life!'

'What do you mean, night of my life?'

The two men looked at each other and laughed.

'Isaac's made arrangements for you to bed down further along the street at the best little cathouse in these parts!'

'Cathouse?' Geoff was appalled. He'd heard tales of what went on in cathouses. They were whorehouses back home and he remembered all his father's scary tales about 'loose' women and the dangers thereof. He'd been most emphatic when Geoff had first left home to go to university and stressed the dangers of disease and learning bad habits. His father would have a heart attack if he knew about this! 'I can't go to no cathouse!' He was shocked at the two men's attitude. It was as if Isaac had bestowed an honour on him.

'Why not?' Somerville asked tersely 'Are you one of those fairy boys?'

'No, of course not! The very idea!'

'Well then? What's the trouble? You'll damn well wish you had when you've not seen a woman for months! We know what that's like, don't we, Shakeshaft?'

The 'breed nodded. 'That we do. Even the sheep look attractive!'

Geoff looked more shocked still.

'You're joking!'

Shakeshaft raised his shoulders in a shrug and walked away. Geoff looked from one to the other.

'Look, fellers, I'm exhausted. All I want is some food and a bed for the night. That's all,' he finished firmly.

Somerville took out a cigarette and lit it. He narrowed his eyes as he looked Geoff over.

'You've never been with a woman, have you? You're scared. You're sweating like a pig!'

Geoff flushed. Now he was embarrassed by Somerville's tone and what he implied. He took a deep breath. What the hell. . . .

'Yes, if you want the truth, I'm scared and going with loose women wasn't part of my education. I was in Edinburgh to study and that's what I did.'

'You must have been a priggish holier-than-thou critter!'

'I did have a girlfiend whom I thought some-day I would marry.'

'So? Didn't you ever . . . ?'

'No, of course not. I respected her. We held hands. I never even kissed her!'

76

'Jesus H Christ! Studying them there medical books must have diluted your blood! It's time you got initiated and by God, Annie and her girls will make a man of you!'

'I don't want—' but Geoff was interrupted.

'Stop whinging about what you don't want! Think of the fun you're going to give those women! Hell! What I would give to be in your boots, and all for free too!' The hot stew was served, and the two men tucked in, but Geoff had lost his appetite.

Then later, after several drinks, the two men escorted an unwilling Geoff down the street and knocked at the door of the biggest establishment in that small town. When the door was opened, they catapulted him into the arms of a couple of women.

'Here he is, Annie. Look after him well and we'll be back for him in the morning!'

FIVE

The door opened and Geoff Potterson stepped outside, taking in a deep breath and looking around him with a new slant on the world. He was now a man. He'd proved himself the night before.

He turned to grin and wave to Annie, the calico queen and her girls. She smiled and waved back as the three girls behind her giggled and puckered their lips at him.

He was much changed. His hair had been cut, his face was now cleanshaven and he smelled of lye soap after the incredible bath and massage they'd given him.

All the stress had been washed away and Annie had plied him with some of her special tequila, which had given him fresh energy and made the sap rise . . .

The night had been long and joyous. The girls had laughed and teased, caressing and giving him a rare chance to study female anatomy. It

78

was breathtaking and he knew now what a fool he would have been to miss this experience.

He'd pleasured all four women, reasoning that it wouldn't be gentlemanly to miss one out. Once initiated, he'd got the knack and there was no stopping him.

Now, though short on sleep, he was ready to face any dangers that might come along.

He hurried along the sidewalk to the saloon where Somerville and Shakeshaft were waiting, speculating on the state the naïve young doc would be in.

They grinned as he came in, face beaming.

'What are you two grinning at?'

Somerville coughed and said jokily,

'Just glad to see you made it. I bet you could eat a dead horse!'

'You've said it! I'll eat anything put in front of me.'

A little later he and the others ate huge beef steaks sizzled over a hot fire and a pile of hash browns and beans washed down with strong coffee.

Then Geoff sat back and belched.

'That was the best feed I've had in a long time!'

'Good,' Somerville said soberly. 'It'll have to last you all day. We're moving out pronto and you've got to get used to this new horse of yours.'

'Hell! I forgot about that. Is he quiet?'

'Well . . . let's say he'll let you mount up!'

'What's that supposed to mean?'

'He's quiet in the sense that he'll let you get astride. After that, is another matter. Some horses fight their riders and then it's a battle between man and beast about who's boss. You're lucky. This horse is a stayer. He could save your life.'

'Well, I suppose I'd better go and introduce myself.'

'We've put the rest of your gear on the pack-animal, at least all you're gonna need. Some of your stuff we traded with Isaac for twenty dollars.' Somerville handed over the cash.

'Is that all I get for all the stuff I brought?'

'You should think yourself lucky you got that! The Cheyenne ruined some of your stuff and it wasn't worth saving. Anyhow, you've got your bedroll, another shirt and some underwear, a pair of boots, and your medical kit and two books. We saw they were important to you and we couldn't make head or tail of them being medical so thought we'd better keep them for you.'

'Thank you very much,' Geoff answered sarcastically. 'You did real well.'

'Let's get on with it then,' said Somerville. 'Let's take him to meet his new buddy. Mordecai called him Charger. I think it was because once you get aboard you've got to hold on tight, because he goes like a rocket!'

Geoff looked appraisingly at the chestnut. He seemed quiet enough. He stood with his head down and Geoff could have sworn he was asleep. He ran his hand tentatively from his head, down in his neck, taking in the strong smell of him.

Shakeshaft stood well back, chewing on a straw. Horses could be unpredictable bastards at times.

'Blow down his nostrils,' Shakeshaft said quietly. Geoff looked at him and wondered whether he was joking but Shakeshaft was serious. The horse's ears twitched.

'I . . . er . . . how should I do that?'

'Keep your hand on him and stand in front of him. Run your hand down his nose and rub him lightly, then get hold of him. Slowly, mind, and blow gently into his nostrils. That way he'll recognize your personal smell. The Cheyenne do that with the wild horses they capture.'

So Geoff did as he was told and though the horse plunged a little, Geoff eventually mounted up and thrust his feet into the heavy iron stirrups, while Somerville hung on to the bridle.

Then both men stood back and waited.

'Now what happens?' Geoff asked nervously as he gripped the reins, so pulling back the animal's head.

'You kick his ribs with your heels to move him on, and you pull on the reins, either left or right,

81

if you want to turn. It's easy,' called Somerville, as Geoff involuntarily kicked.

The horse took off at a gallop down the street, the wind in Geoff's face and the ground beneath him rushing by at an alarming speed.

His heart in his mouth, Geoff hung on grimly. Then he found that the rocking motion under him was eased when he put his weight on the wide iron stirrups. It was like standing, with the horse stretching out under him.

Soon, they were passing the cathouse. The girls out on the upper veranda yelled and waved at him in encouragement. He pulled on the reins until Charger slowed to a walk, then he experimented by riding in a figure of eight, pulling on both left and right reins until he reckoned he'd got the knack.

So, he would show those two hairy-heeled frontiersmen that he wasn't such a fool as they thought. He knew what had been in their minds. They'd wanted to see him thrown. He'd show them!

He kicked Charger hard in the ribs and was ready when the horse took a mighty leap and raced back down the road, but when he came abreast of the watching men, Charger stopped of his own accord and dug his fore-hoofs into the earth, stiff-legged. Geoff flew on over the horse's neck and landed heavily.

He heard a peal of laughter as he lay half-conscious, wondering what he'd done wrong. Then he was being heaved to his feet.

He shook his head as the world tilted crazily.

'You all right?' Somerville was supporting him.

'Yes . . . I think so.' He became conscious of Shakeshaft on his other side.

'Then you'd better get back on and show the bastard who's boss!'

'Must I?'

But Shakeshaft didn't answer. Both men counted aloud,

'One . . . two . . . and over!'

Geoff, still dazed, was back in the saddle. In a panic he grabbed the reins, thrust his feet into the stirrups and this time only touched Charger's ribs gently. He was amazed when the animal moved slowly ahead as docile as if he had not an ounce of passion in him.

'See, it's easy,' called Somerville, grinning at Shakeshaft. 'Just treat him right, and he'll be eating out of your hand in no time.'

Geoff experimented and found that a kick a touch harder set the horse to a trot, while a touch on the bridle stopped him or turned him left or right. Soon Geoff was enjoying the feeling of growing power over the animal and the sense of freedom and movement.

At the end, when he dismounted, Charger rubbed his head against Geoff's arm and a new bond was forged, never to be broken.

'You did real well,' Somerville approved. 'I think we can safely say you'll do. I think you need a drink. What d'you say?'

Geoff agreed heartily. He was beginning to get a liking for this American whiskey.

As they sat over their drinks, Somerville brought up the question of Geoff's proficiency with a gun. Geoff was uneasy.

'I've never used a handgun. Once or twice during the Christmas break back home, Father went shooting grouse on the moors and I went as a beater. Once or twice he let me have a shot at the grouse with his gun. Of course I missed but it was fun.'

'Fun? You don't call shooting fun in these parts,' roared Somerville. 'Hell's bells! You've got to learn to shoot and as soon as possible. We've got you a Colt forty-five and Mordecai's throwing in the Spencer and ammo because of your treatment to his arm. As soon as we find a nice quiet place for you to practise, we'll put you through your paces. A feller doesn't get the reputation as a gunman without a hell of a lot of practise! It's a profession, you know. A keen eye can save your life. Or you can trade your skill as a bounty hunter or someone's bodyguard. The pay's good!'

'I'm not likely to do any of that. I'm a doctor, a healer, not a killer!'

'You've got to be everything out here, Doc, so

84

keep open-minded. There's a different set of rules out here from way back where you come from. We're all primitive people and the only way to survive is to be all things to all men!'

'You really mean that? I must reap and sow, become a cowpoke if necessary, build my own home if I want one, as well as do what I do best?'

'Now you've got the right idea, Doc. If you have to kill a man, you'll kill him, just like the rest of us. You're no better than we are!'

Geoff emptied his glass and poured another drink. Suddenly his whole life had changed.

Without warning, the batwings of the saloon burst open and a man stood in the gap, panting and spent. He smelled of sweat and fear.

'The Jayhawkers are coming up the trail with a massive herd, nearly a mile wide. They're devastating the country of all grass and they're heading this way!'

'Goddammit!' the barman roared. 'The sons of bitches will have to be stopped! I'll tell the boss! Get yourself a drink while I'm gone.' He shoved a bottle and glass across the bar as the man staggered in and hung over the plank bar. He poured the rotgut and drank greedily.

Geoff watched fascinated.

'Who are the Jayhawkers?' Somerville and Shakeshaft were already looking to their six-shooters and looking grim.

'They hang out on both sides of the Rio Grande. They buy Mexican cattle at a cut price and they bring 'em up through Texas. Then they try to hit the Chisholm Trail and come on into the new territories with the idea of flooding the market back East with cheap cattle.'

'Well, what's bad about that? Folks would welcome cheap beef.'

'The trouble is, Doc, that those cattle have ticks and so do the Texan longhorns. If the army knows that a herd is coming up, and they will, never fear, that means we'll have soldiers on our tracks, you can bet on it!'

'Why will they do that?'

'Because, Doc, they'll know an American and a 'breed have passed this way and the army would as soon kill two birds with one stone as not! We'll have to get out pronto!'

Isaac Sloane came out of his office with the barman and went to question the newcomer. Yes, the man said, they're less than a day's ride away and are being chivvied along as fast as they can go, and yes, they're the same Mex *bandidos* who tried to hit the trail last year and caused such havoc crossing Mordecai Sloane's northern range.

'There's no time to lose,' bellowed Isaac. 'Maria! Get out here fast!'

When the girl came running, looking startled, he shouted at her roughly to move her legs fast and go and tell Uncle Mordecai to get himself here pronto.

Geoff protested.

'Mr Sloane, your brother must rest. He's in no condition—'

'Rubbish!' barked Isaac. 'He's not some mealy-mouthed city gent! He'll not let his lack of arm stop him from what he must do! He's got a son out there managing his ranch and a healthy herd of cattle to protect!'

So it was, for not long afterwards Mordecai arrived with Marie. He looked white and drawn but surprisingly fit for a man who'd just had his arm sawn off.

'What is it, Isaac? Marie here had a fire up her backside. Where's the fire?'

'Sit down, Mord. You're not going to like this, but the Jayhawkers are coming again.'

Mordecai sat down heavily.

'Hell and blast! Are they coming up the same old trail?'

'Yeah.' Isaac nodded to the messenger. 'Come and tell Mord what you told me.'

Mordecai listened, running a hand over bristly chin as he did so.

'So the bastards mean to run those cursed cattle through Long Ridge Gap and on to my range. Jamie with his men won't be able to turn 'em back. We'll have to send him reinforce-ments. At least this time we've had warning. Last time, they were on us before we knew what was happening.'

'If they get through, they'll eat the grazing and leave their ticks behind and you know how long it took to get rid of the pesky devils.'

'Too right. This time they'll have to be stopped for good.'

'So what do you suggest, Mord?'

'We'll send out runners to the other ranches to meet at the head of the pass. I've a few barrels of dynamite stashed at the store. We'll blow up the neck of the pass!'

'But Mord, we can't do that! How will we get from one range to another if we blow up the pass?'

'Easy. We'll use enough dynamite to block the narrow neck and afterwards dig out the rubble. All we want is to spook the herd so that it turns on itself and those which don't die will head back at a mad lick and, with luck, overrun the bastards driving them.'

Isaac considered and then laughed.

'It might just work. It'll mean just the right amount of dynamite to do the job. But who have we got who's skilled enough to know just how much to use?'

'I have the skill.' They all looked at Somerville. 'I'll set the charges for you. I was trained in explosives before I came to my last posting.'

88

'By God, if you can do it, we'll be in your debt for ever,' Mordecai enthused. 'You and that there doc sure are lifesavers!'

Geoff watched and waited. This was a situation he'd never expected in his wildest dreams. He felt helpless, swept along by events not under his control.

'So we'd better get moving,' Isaac reckoned. 'We'll get along to the sheriff and put out a call for a posse. There's no time to lose!'

The men of the town were more than willing to volunteer. Mordecai Sloane's store was a life-line. He wasn't a man to cross but when a man showed loyalty he could be very generous indeed.

Shakeshaft volunteered to ride ahead and scout the country. Pointedly he asked Geoff to accompany him.

'A chance to get used to that there horse of yours. I'll give you a quick demonstration of the use of your firearms. Unfortunately there's no time for you to hit any targets but if you know how to load up and pull the triggers, it might be useful.'

So Geoff got a rough idea of how to handle both rifle and handgun, with orders to aim a little lower as a start, for greenhorns' reflexes always jerked the muzzle upwards.

'Aim for a feller's chest or the middle of his back, and if you're lucky and not cross-eyed,

you'll do for him,' Shakeshaft said calmly.
'Here's a knife for you for if you have to cut
someone's throat on the quiet!'

Geoff swallowed a hard lump in his throat. His
heart pounded with horror at what Shakeshaft's
words conjured up.

'I can't see myself in a position where I'll be
cutting a man's throat!'

Shakeshaft smiled cynically at him.

'Out here, Doc, you take events as they come.
You're not just a doctor, you're a man and a
survivor. Now, lets's pack some essentials, load
up and we'll be on our way.'

Shakeshaft seemed to know by instinct which
trails to follow. He explained that he was using
old Indian trails now forgotten by white men,
but the indications were still there for an Indian
to read.

After four hours' uncomfortable riding, Geoff
eventually got the knack of moving with the
same rhythm as Charger. His lower spine ached
but he was proud of himself. They'd taken a
break earlier in a small canyon and Shakeshaft
had taken the time to give him some shooting
practice. He'd been surprisingly good and
Shakeshaft reckoned that now he had a fifty-fifty
chance of surviving in the wilderness.

'Only fifty-fifty?' Geoff was disappointed. He
was proud of his new skill.

'Hell, Doc, pulling a trigger and hitting a

target doesn't mean you're an instant *pistolero*! It takes years of practice and your reflexes have to be faster than the other man's! Oh boy! Just wait until we hit trouble and you'll see for yourself!'

'You think these Jayhawkers will stand and fight?'

'Wouldn't you, if you had real money invested and you saw your investment turning on itself and stampeding to its death? Those Jayhawkers are going to be spitting mad once they see what's happening . . . if they're lucky, that is. Chances are some of 'em will be killed in the first rush of steers, but there'll be the big boys following on behind. There'll be a counter attack and then all hell will break loose.'

Geoff reached for more coffee. His hand trembled a little as he poured. He hoped to God Shakeshaft was wrong but in his heart he knew the 'breed knew what he was talking about.

At early dawn next day Shakeshaft spied the grey haze on the horizon. Without a word he pulled up and pointed.

'What is it, Shakeshaft?'

They were now through the pass and standing on a promontory. Before them lay a stretch of fertile grassland, the grass now turning to a golden hay.

'See the skyline? See the haze? That's dust raised by the herd we're waiting for. See how far it stretches widthways? In less than four hours we'll see them narrowing to a V and the point riders will hedge the leaders in so that they come through the pass maybe fifty abreast.'

'What should we do?'

'Wait until we see how many riders are coming into the pass with them, then we ride like hell back to the point where we can signal the others who'll be waiting. After that, we'll have to find ourselves a safe hide or we might get caught up in the blast which follows.' He grinned. 'You don't think Somerville will have been twiddling his thumbs? He'll have been back there, fixing his dynamite and oh boy! Does he make a good job of it!'

'You've seen him in action before?'

'Yeah. The colonel got him to rig up a charge a few years ago when some outlaws holed up in some mountain caves and it was a stalemate. The colonel thought he could starve 'em out but it appeared they had water and provisions. So, he got sick of waiting and Somerville shinned up that mountain side all on his own, taking all the gear with him. Some feat. Then, we who were waiting at a safe distance watched him scramble down in a mighty hurry and before we could count to ten, the whole world seemed to explode. Rocks and dirt was flung into the air and the whole of that goddamn mountain was changed for ever! We never found one body to bury. That was it. Finished.' He shook his head.

'I'm not sure whether he's right about the pass. He says we can dig out the debris and open the pass again. I'm not so sure about that.'

'What happens if its blocked for ever?'

'The locals will have to find another trail into Mexico and Mordecai Sloane might find he's lost some of his range.'

It was as Shakeshaft predicted; the cattle, urged on by outriders, pressed on and gradually the leaders forged ahead and came into plain view. They counted at least a dozen riders controlling the herd, some engaged in rounding up strays and more determined mavericks. There was the occasional sound of gunfire far back of the herd as if to hurry on the laggards.

Shakeshaft took a long drink from his canteen and handed it to Geoff.

'Drink your fill. We've got a hell of a long way to go!' Then they were retracing their tracks. When on flat straight ground again, Shakeshaft gave the old Indian war cry and his mount lengthened his stride into a gallop. Geoff closed his eyes, kicked Charger and hung on grimly as they made for the signalling point.

At last the nightmare ride was over. Geoff sank to the ground as Shakeshaft climbed up on to a needle of rock, produced a mirror and directed its reflected light back along the widened pass to a landmark known as Devil's Leap. After a few minutes an answering light shone back.

93

Relieved, Shakeshaft rejoined the doctor, only to find him asleep on the ground. He kicked him lightly with his boot.

'Hey, Doc, wake up! We've got to get to hell out of here, pronto!'

'Wha . . . what's that?'

'Jesus Christ! Get up! We haven't any time to waste! Those steers will be well on their way through the pass now and by God, Somerville won't be sitting on his arse. That dynamite will pop soon and we'd best get ourselves as far away as possible!'

That brought Geoff wide awake. He hadn't realized he'd fallen asleep. He'd only relaxed for a minute.

'OK. Where now?'

'See that line of hills over there? There's Indian burial caves. I've never been in them but the old folk used to talk about sacred rites and ceremonies. If we can reach them we'll be safe from anything Somerville can come up with.'

So, wearily, Geoff mounted up and they picked their way over rough ground. Geoff found it best to let Charger find his own way. He was a sure-footed beast and Geoff was coming to trust him more and more.

Shakeshaft led the way, saying little, but he urged Geoff on when his mount faltered. Soon they came to the foot of the crag where now Geoff could see a grim line of rocks with scrub covering part of the loose shale. Now it took all their time to persuade the horses to tackle the incline and they struggled, sometimes slipping backwards. But eventually they reached a flat stratum of rock, where they dismounted and led the horses along a narrow path running around the crag.

They stabled the horses in the first cave they came to. Both horses panicked a little as they were led into the dark depths but, speaking encouragingly and stroking the animals to calm them, they managed to tie them safely to protruding needles of rock.

When Geoff's eyes adjusted to the gloom, he saw that there were signs of occupation. There were bones and rubbish, the remains of discarded food and the ashes of a long-dead fire. But there was no time to stand and stare for Shakeshaft urged him on.

'Come on, Doc, we'll climb higher to the ceremonial caves where we can look out and see what's happening.'

Geoff followed Shakeshaft along the narrowing path. He moved cautiously, for now they had to hug the rock and move step by step. Geoff, taking one look down, felt dizzy and closed his eyes as he felt his way along the rough rock. Once, a bird flew out of a crevice in front of Shakeshaft and he cursed luridly, but he moved on until at last he stepped up on to a shelf of rock. There before them were the openings of three caves, not very large openings; they would easily be missed by those riding through the pass down below.

Geoff joined Shakeshaft, who was staring far below in the direction of where Somerville would be now. He hoped he might detect some movement but all was still.

'You think he's in place?' Geoff asked when he'd got over his dizziness.

'Knowing him, I'd bet my last dollar on it. Let's take a look around. I've always been curious about this place but because I had a white man for a father I was never allowed to come on a pilgrimage.' He laughed bitterly. 'The Cheyenne think a 'breed contaminates everything he touches, even his woman!'

Geoff heard the sadness in his voice and didn't answer. He followed Shakeshaft into the largest of the caves and saw for the first time the painted Indian murals going back thousands of years. He saw the hunters hunting buffalo and deer, women grinding corn and cooking on fires on which were heavy iron pots. There were drawings of the sun god and of the god of rain and of the earth and he only wished he had time to study them closer.

He saw too that there was a mound of stones at the back of the cave and that by some strange chance there was a crack in the rock. A ray of light beamed down and he guessed it must be an altar.

Then as he was staring at it, something happened that neither of them expected. A figure hurtled from behind the rock altar and leapt up on Shakeshaft's back. He was only a moving shadow in the corner of Geoff's eye but his reflex was fast. He saw Shakeshaft fall help-lessly beneath the Indian brave, his body writhing as he tried to free himself. Geoff saw the hand rise above Shakeshaft's head and the glint of a knife coming down in a purposeful chopping movement. He flung himself forward as he'd done many times as a teenager in the playing-fields of his school during rugby matches. He tackled the squirming figure, who smelt of rancid buffalo fat.

The knife grazed Shakeshaft's shoulder and clattered to the ground as the brave turned like a snake to battle it out with Geoff. Geoff saw the murderous hatred in the man's eyes as they came together. Instinctively, Geoff's fists came up in the good old boxing style, taking the man by surprise. Geoff heard the crack of the jawbone and felt a rush of elation, but it was short-lived as the Indian came at him, head down and arms flailing.

They struggled back and forth. At last the brave managed to grab his knife; leaping to his feet and with legs bent he came at Geoff with a howl of rage. It was then that Geoff lost control of himself. To hell with rules! This was life and death stuff. He gave a rousing yell of his own, a yell that would have brought any Scots clan running. He closed with this devil incarnate, putting his head down and lifting the squirming body above his head. He paused to take a breath, swung him around, then let go and watched him hurtle over the side of the cliff. His scream could be heard growing fainter and fainter, and Geoff leaned against the wall of the cave and was sick.

He'd sent a man to his death.

SIX

'You allright?' Shakeshaft's voice sounded croaky. Geoff pulled himself together, remembering that Shakeshaft was injured and his medical training kicked in. He would deal with the problem of the dead man later. Swiftly he moved to crouch down beside the scout, who was holding his shoulder. Blood dripped from his fingers.

'Yes,' he answered briefly, then: 'I'll have to tear away that sleeve and look at that wound.

Shakeshaft, looking as though he was in pain, did not object and with several tugs at the hand-stitching of the Indian-made jerkin, Geoff exposed the injury. The knife had gouged a slice of flesh from the shoulder muscle. It gaped open and Geoff pursed his lips. 'This wound should be properly cleaned. I'll go down and bring up my medical bag—'

'No!' It took effort but Shakeshaft was vehement. 'Just look in my jerkin pocket and you'll find a small flask of whiskey. Empty some of it over the wound and give me the rest.'

'But—'

'Just goddamn do as I say! Then go and bring a bunch of that lichen growing on that wall and bunch it up and stick it on the wound. Go on!' As Geoff stared astonished he went on wearily: 'Look, the Indians have been using lichen for years to stem bleeding.'

Geoff did as he was told. Then he bound up Shakeshaft's shoulder with a couple of strips torn from a not over-clean shirt.

He worried that Shakeshaft would die of blood-poisoning.

After it was over, Shakeshaft drank what was left in the bottle and belched.

'I'll be fine tomorrow,' he began. Then there came a mighty explosion which shook the cave floor. Several rocks were displaced and Geoff ran to the mouth of the cave. There he saw the devastation down below. The whole panoramic view had changed. Dirt and debris polluted the clear air, the narrow neck of the pass was a jumble of rocks.

Shakeshaft dragged himself up to view the sight. He swayed a little, despite his attempt at bravado.

'So he did it,' he said softly. 'The lucky bastard really did it!' He began to laugh.

Geoff shook him. 'Hold on now, control your-self! Or you're going to set off the bleeding again.'

Something in Geoff's voice made Shakeshaft give him a sharp look. Yes, this young greenhorn was rapidly turning into a real man. Was it because he'd sent another man to his death? He needed to find out. He sobered quickly.

'How many men you reckon lie down there amongst the steers?' he asked carefully.

'For God's sake, Shakeshaft, I don't know! The Lord have mercy on their souls!'

'What about the Cheyenne you flung over the cliff?'

Geoff shuddered, remembering. 'How do you know he was a Cheyenne?'

'Because he was my wife's brother.'

Geoff looked at him with shock.

'Her brother? Oh, my god!'

'Don't worry about it. I shan't. He's been out to get me for years and must have followed us and guessed where we would make for when we headed towards the sacred caves. He must have climbed down the crevice over the altar. It was a known place of entry.'

They gazed solemnly down at the devastation below. A cloud haze of dust was slowly drifting away.

'Those Jayhawkers sure got a mighty surprise. I reckon they'll make a run for it back over the river . . . what's left of 'em,' Shakeshaft mused.

'Maybe Somerville and the boys have plans to go after them. I guess we'd better get back and report what we've seen. Whatever Somerville decides to do there's sure to be a celebration tonight!'

They backtracked, but now they could move more quickly as they relaxed their vigilance. Nothing stirred except for the odd panting lizard basking on sun-heated rocks.

They heard the gunfire well before they came to the rendezvous. At first Shakeshaft cursed. Had the leading Jayhawkers outwitted them? But no, it was Mordecai Sloane's son and his crew who were drinking and letting off their guns in an early celebration.

Somerville's face was like thunder.

'Goddamn fools! Some son of a bitch brought a barrel of booze along with the dynamite and young Sloane can't control the bastards. Anyhow, enough of that. Tell us about the explosion.'

'You did a mighty fine job, Somerville,' Shakeshaft enthused. 'Took down nearly the whole cliff and buried more than half the herd, I reckon, with the men running point.' Then he became serious. 'God knows whether the pass will ever be opened up again. It was a mighty bang.'

Somerville grinned sheepishly.

'I think I maybe overdid it. It's a few years

since I worked in demolition but I wanted to be sure. Did you see anyone escape?'

Shakeshaft shook his head and spat on the ground.

'Never saw no one, but we had a bit of trouble of our own!'

'Oh? And what was that?'

'Cheyenne trouble,' Shakeshaft answered briefly. 'He's crowbait now thanks to Doc here. The son of a bitch jumped me. He must have been following us and he sliced my arm instead of my throat. Doc here took him on ... he's good with his fists, by the way, and in the end he threw him over the cliff. It happened just before the big bang, so we can't be dead sure no one got out alive.'

Somerville nodded and looked at Geoff with new respect. He held out his hand. Geoff shook it.

'Good man!'

He looked at Shakeshaft's shoulder.

'He fixed you up right, then?'

'Yep. Cool as a dripping icicle in spring.'

'Then, Doc, would you mind taking a look at one of Sloane's crew? His horse slipped and the feller shunted out of the saddle. He was dragged quite a ways before we could stop the frightened animal. I think he's maybe put his hip out. His ankle is blown up like a balloon.'

'I'll take a look.'

Geoff found the cowboy lying in the shelter of some rocks. He was groaning and lying in a twisted heap. It didn't take long to examine him and Geoff knew he could do nothing for the man out here with no real equipment.

He straightened up. Shakeshaft's eyes were on him.

'We'll have to make some kind of stretcher to take him back to town.'

Shakeshaft nodded. 'I'll see to it. The Indians make a travois from larch poles. They're quick and easy to make and his own horse will pull it. It'll be a rough ride but we'll get him home.'

Geoff watched with interest as Shakeshaft directed two of the injured man's buddies to cut down three young saplings, trim them off, then make the travois. They used two horse blankets bound on to the poles with tough vines and so fashioned a rough kind of stretcher. Geoff marvelled at the speed with which the whole thing was made.

Then came the slow ride back to the small community, the patient comatose from a shot of laudanum that Geoff adminstered.

Once back home, the revellers carried on drinking. They shouldered a protesting Somerville and hailed him as their saviour. They pressed liquor on him and cheered as he drank shuddering at the potent spirit.

104

Geoff watched uneasily. The womenfolk were joining in and the only help he got with his patient's hip was an old toothless woman who was surprisingly competent.

'Aye, I've been birthing babies and tying up wounds for the past forty years,' she cackled. 'This feller's no different from the rest!' The noise and uproar outside the mean hut they were in left her unmoved. 'They've got to bust loose sometimes, those young 'uns. There's not much joy in these parts, God knows, so they know how to enjoy theirselves!'

It was nearly dawn before the last reveller collapsed where he fell and slept.

The small town was quiet. The townsfolk and the visiting cowboys were still hung over. Geoff watched a straggle of women make their way to the public well for water; they too looked as if they'd had a rough night. There was the distant cry of a child no doubt hungry and its mother still sleeping.

Geoff watched grimly from his hut. He'd just checked on his patient and knew he could now leave him in the old woman's hands. He would go and find Somerville. No doubt the ex-officer would be hung over too. He had no idea where Shakeshaft was. He'd seemed to have disappeared during the revelry.

He found Somerville down at the stream plunging his head in the icy-cold water, then shaking himself like some prairie dog. Geoff laughed, relieved.

'So you made it! I thought you would still be paralytic!'

Somerville grinned.

'It takes more than·what those sons of bitches poured down my throat to lay me out! I've got steel guts!'

Geoff followed his example and though a scream rose in his throat at the shock of cold water, felt better afterwards.

Then, to their consternation they heard gunfire. Geoff sprang to his feet as Somerville swivelled to look back at the huddle of buildings behind them.

'What the hell ... Are the fools drinking again?' asked Geoff, shocked and bewildered.

'No,' answered Somerville grimly. 'It's what I dreaded. Those goddamn Jayhawkers found the skyline trail and while these bastards have celebrated, they've spent the night coming after us! We'd better get back, pronto!'

But they were too late. The riders were already pouring into the town, racing round and round, firing at anything that moved.

The two men ran and took cover behind some rocks. Geoff could hear Somerville curse as they watched the savage onslaught.

Panic set in. The menfolk, galvanized to action from the noise automatically spilled out

106

from their homes, firing, but they were being gunned down like rats in a trap. The circle of riders was growing smaller as the men moved in. Cowboys who'd spent the night in the open or in the outhouses came under fire and Geoff saw men shot and collapse and lie still. Then from the edge of town a lone shack went up in flames. The marauders had chosen well, for the wind blew the flames towards the other wooden huts. Before his very eyes Geoff saw the sheets of flames streak along the straggling street. He watched women come screaming out of the flamelit houses, some carrying small children. All were shot down.

'We've got to do something,' he gasped to Somerville who was staring in horror at the spectacle.

'Like what?'

'What about that dynamite in Sloane's store?'

'How in hell can we get there? It'll be on fire soon and then the whole lot will go up!'

'Jesus! We must do something!'

Somerville looked helplessly at him.

'Look, Doc, there's a time to fight and a time to stand back. We can't help those lying dead out there. Those Jayhawkers have to return to where they came from. We'll have to contact the army and go after them. That's all we can do.'

Geoff watched the riders, noting that there

were Mexicans in sombreros amongst the white Americanos, all bristling with repeating rifles and bandoleers. Someone amongst them was supplying them with all the latest weapons. This mob were well organized.

He saw the leader raise his rifle and wave. On impulse, Geoff left his safe hiding-place and scrambled up the rocks away from the stream towards where the man sat on his horse. He was full of rage as he closed in behind his target. Somerville watched from their hiding-place. What was the hothead trying to achieve? He would surely be shot down!

Geoff took his time as the man sat watching the mayhem. His enjoyment was evident as his booming laughter rang out. Inch by inch, adrenaline flowing at the anticipation of what he was about to do, he closed in for the kill.

Dispassionately, his eyes roamed over his target noting the criss-crossed bandoleers; the man was a veritable arsenal, the arrogant neck of him, the wide shoulders under the sheepskin jerkin and the wide sombrero giving him the appearance of an exotic mushroom.

Then Geoff took a deep breath, coldly remembered Somerville's instructions about aiming low because of the upward swing of this gun's barrel and fired.

The bullet struck a second before the explosion that rocked Geoff back on his heels. He was conscious of Somerville scrambling up behind him as he watched, as if in slow motion, the rise of the body from the horse, crimson staining the man's back, and then the wild plunging of the horse as the rider hit the ground.

Then Somerville was dragging him away to lie flat under a straggly bush that was no real protection.

'Hell's bells, you did it!' marvelled Somerville. 'There'll be hell to pay when those bastards realize their boss is dead!'

Geoff was shaking. He'd never in his life ever dreamed he might shoot a man in the back. He couldn't speak but bellied his way after Somerville into the shelter of the rocks to wait and watch.

The reaction came sooner than they expected. One rider galloped up, leading his boss's horse, and saw the body on the ground. He dismounted, crouched and turned the body over. Then he stood up and gave a shrill whistle. At once two figures galloped out of the smoke. They halted beside the man and the body, then they all turned to look at the near-barren landscape.

This was when Somerville put a warning hand on Geoff.

'Lie perfectly still and they might not cotton on to us. But they're no fools. I think we might be in for a chase!' He nodded to a jagged crevice in the hard ground a few feet from where they were hidden. 'You reckon you could roll into that there crack and inch your way along it as fast as you can?'

Geoff was a big man. If he got stuck, his chances would be nil. Somerville was the smaller of the two.

'Maybe you should go first. If I stick, you'll not get the chance to escape.'

'Not a chance. You're nearer than me, so don't argue but be on your way. If the worst comes to the worst I'll hold them back with fire.' Cooly, he proceeded to load up his sixgun. 'I only wish I'd carried my rifle to that damned stream, but I wasn't actually at my brightest! Now off with you and good luck!'

Geoff took a deep breath and began his crawl. He moved slowly and the bush hid him from view as he inched his way to the opening in the ground. It stretched for quite a way but Geoff had no means of knowing how deep it was. He had to take a chance, drop into it and hope for the best.

He managed to flop into the gash in the ground. It was wider than he expected and he fell with a dull thud on to dirt and rock and the remains of a dead animal. The smell was nauseating but he wasn't really aware of it for his spine still crawled with the thought that a bullet could crash into him at any moment.

He found himself sweating. He wanted to lie there until he got his strength back but knew he had to wriggle on because of Somerville following behind.

Suddenly there came yells and shots just before Somerville crashed down behind him. The ex-officer had been rumbled. Geoff struggled to his feet. Looking back, he saw the three men covering the ground at a fast lick, guns firing and bullets flying all around them. Geoff took a gamble as Somerville crawled rapidly towards him, taking a chance, rising up from the crack and emptying his gun into the bunch of men. He saw one man fall but the others came on.

Now Somerville was on his feet and he too was firing haphazardly. There was no time to aim, just to launch a hail of bullets. Geoff felt a sharp pain in his arm, as if he'd been stung by a hornet. He saw that Somerville was bleeding from a wound in the head, but he kept on firing until his gun was empty. Another man fell, while the third man backed off, and started running to his hobbled horse. Geoff loaded up again and sent a shot after him but missed. The bastard would alert the rest of the band and even he, Geoff, knew that they could never survive an organized hunt.

'Let's get out of here,' Somerville barked, mopping at his head with a dirty bandanna.

'We'll head downstream in the water. They'll miss our tracks that way. They'll waste time hunting up and down stream for our spoor. It's our only chance!' He started to run back towards the river, Geoff following.

Somerville didn't waste time looking at the fast-flowing stream. He jumped in and Geoff saw the current sweeping him away quite fast. Taking a deep breath, Geoff followed suit and instinctively tried to swim. His clothes were heavy and he was gasping with the shock of icy water engulfing him. He thrashed wildly as he rolled over and over in the tumbling water which carried him swiftly downstream. He started to pray. He'd long forgotten his Weslyan teaching but now it came back in full force.

Vaguely he was aware of Somerville's body being tossed around, but protruding rocks in the water were his main concern. Water rippled over them and he took some bruising as he bumped into them before being swept onwards.

Then, without warning, a lariat curled about one shoulder and a raised arm. He felt the rope tighten and begin to pull him against the current. It was like an answer to his prayer.

The water buffeted him as he was drawn to the bank, then welcome hands were dragging him from the water. He lay on his back, spent, and looked up into the grim face of Shakeshaft.

'You . . .' he said weakly and began to cough up water.

Shakeshaft rolled him on his belly and pounded him between the shoulder blades while he vomited more water. At last he stopped spewing and took several deep breaths.

'Somerville . . . what of him?' he managed to gasp.

'Don't worry about him. He's got the luck of the devil. He was clinging on to an overhanging tree-branch when my friend here saw him and we come down to drag him out. That's when we saw you come tumbling over and over like some dead steer. You sure were lucky, Doc.'

'I'll say. You saved my life, Shakeshaft. I'll not forget it.'

Shakeshaft grinned. 'I can save your life still further before you catch your death of pneumonia. Here, take a swig of this.' He held out his liquor flask. Never had whiskey tasted so good. 'Now we'll have to get you out of those wet clothes. We'll wrap you in a horse blanket and we'll hang your stuff on a rack over a fire like we've done with Somerville's. It'll dry in no time.'

So Geoff sat huddled in a blanket along with Somerville and watched the flames leap up. High above the flames, the hot air rising fast, were the clothes, like a line of washing, Geoff thought. It was amazing what these frontiersmen could cope with. Later, wearing still slightly damp clothes, Geoff was introduced properly to Shakeshaft's companion.

'This is Billie Joe, a scout along of me with the lieutenant's troop. He never went along with the sentence the colonel gave Somerville. He's a good buddy.'

Geoff looked at the dark, chiselled face before him. He too was of mixed blood and guessed he could be part Mexican. The man nodded gravely at him.

'Any friend of Shakeshaft's a friend of mine.' He held his hand out for Geoff to shake.

'I must thank you too, for saving me,' Geoff replied.

Billie Joe shrugged.

'I understand you're a doctor. Some day you might save me!'

Then Geoff heard that the troop was in the area, that they were still hunting Somerville but had been ordered to take part in the fight against the Jayhawkers when the large herd of steers had been sighted coming over the Rio Grande. The telegraph wires had been busy relaying news back and forth from Fort Santos to Fort Blaine. Three divisions had been deployed to hunt down the Jayhawkers and take on the task of turning the herd on itself and whipping them back across the river.

But to their commander's surprise, the job had been done for them. Someone somewhere had dynamited the pass and the panicked herd, which had not been caught up in the blast, had turned on itself in a stampede that had resulted in a monstrous mound of carcasses piled high. Only a few dozen stray animals were left to round up. The commander was pleased and puzzled. Who had planted the explosive?

Billie Joe looked at Somerville in a knowing manner.

'You're an expert on explosives.'

Somerville grinned. 'You damn well know I am!'

Billie Joe nodded and put a finger to the side of his nose.

'I hear nothing and I see nothing!

'Then you're a goddamn poor scout!' They both laughed.

Shakeshaft stood up, shading his eyes to look back at the haze.

'So what happened back there?'

Somerville filled him in as to what had happened after the celebration, the coming of the Jayhawkers and the firing of the town.

'So we'd better go back and clean up,' Shakeshaft said soberly. 'There might be some wounded for Doc here to look to . . .'

'My medical equipment!' gasped Geoff,

115

suddenly remembering that it was in the old woman's hut along with his patient. That brought him wide awake and raring to go. He took another swig from Shakeshaft's flask and when Shakeshaft suggested riding double, he sprang up behind the scout as if used to it from birth. Somerville followed behind Billie Joe and they made good time back to the ruined town, which was still smoking, the air choking with fumes.

Amazingly, there were still outlying shacks not consumed by fire. A few men and women were milling helplessly around, coming cautiously out of hiding-places now that the mayhem was over. A woman with two small children emerged from a soddy, half-dug into the ground and used as a cold storehouse in summer. It was nothing but a deep pit braced with timbers and grass sods used for a roof. The Jayhawkers had ignored it and it had saved the lives of the mother and children.

The work of moving the dead bodies was under way. The few dead Jayhawkers were thrown into a cesspit but the bodies of the towns-folk, men and women, were being taken to the little cemetery, to be buried as soon as possible because of the heat.

Geoff hurried to the old woman's hut which was still standing though one corner of it was scorched as if the fire had been extinguished

116

before it took off. He pushed open the creaky door and his eyes pierced the gloom.

'Make a move, mister and you're dead!' croaked a hoarse voice. When Geof's eyes had accustomed themselves, he saw the old woman crouched by his patient's bed, clutching a rusty shotgun. She looked bone-weary.

'It's me, Doc Potterson. Remember?'

The shotgun clattered to the floor as the old woman sagged forward. Geoff sprang to catch her as she fell to the floor.

He lifted her up gently. She was crying and clutching him close.

'Oh, thank God you're here! I managed to put the fire out but it took all the water I got! I heard the shooting and the screams and I came back here. I don't know what's been happening outside. You nearly got it, Doc. I was ready to shoot.' She started to laugh hysterically.

Geoff slapped her lightly on the cheek.

'Get a hold on yourself, Mary. You're brave and strong. Don't give way!'

She stared up at him, fingering her cheek.

'You hit me!'

'I'm sorry. I had to do it, Mary.' He shook her gently. 'Tell me about the patient. Is he dead?' He looked over to the still form on the narrow truckle bed.

'No.' Mary drew herself up with an effort, pride in her voice. 'I gave him a dose of your laudanum when the fighting broke out and I saw that they were firing our homes.' She shuddered. 'I thought it would only be a question of time before we went up in flames. I knew I couldn't move him so I thought I'd give him some of your laudanum and he wouldn't know what was happening. I hope I did right, Doc?'

'Quite right, Mary.' He patted her arm and went over to the still figure. The patient was still sleeping. 'You gave him quite a shot!'

'I wasn't sure about the dose. I hope to God it wasn't too much!'

'He'll sleep through it. Now where's my medical bag?' He looked around but couldn't see a sign of it. 'And my books?'

'All safe, Doc. I put them where I put my valuables, under the hearthstone yonder.' She tottered across the floor to the flat stone in front of the open hearth and began to tug at it. Geoff hastened to help her and saw that underneath was a shallow pit.

Once it was opened, he saw that down below was his bag and his books, along with a Bible, Prayer Book and a rusty tin box. Mary reached in and clutched the box to her breast.

'Thank God, everything's safe! I reckoned that if the place burned, someone would find this cache of stuff intact. I'd rather my mother's gold ring and her locket went to someone who would value them than they be destroyed for ever.'

Carefully she opened the box. She lifted out the locket and held it out for Geoff to see.

'Why don't you wear it?' asked Geoff 'It's beautiful, and the ring, why not get the pleasure from them?'

She looked at him with derision.

'Doc, you have no idea what life really is, do you? If I'd worn my ring and the locket, I'd not have them now. Some son of a bitch would have come along and taken them from me! There's been times in my life when I've seen the very worst in men, but I've survived! No man has ever broken my heart! I would never allow it!'

Geoff was moved. This woman was about his mother's age if she'd lived, but she would have had a better-sheltered life than this woman would ever dream of. He put an arm about her and kissed the top of her head.

'You're a gem, Mary!'

Her eyes glowed and she gave him a tremulous smile as her weathered cheek flushed.

'I've never had a compliment in years and never such a gentlemanly one,' she told him happily.

'Now, I think we'll both go and see what we can do to help those who survived. There'll be much organizing to do and I think you could take charge of the womenfolk and chidren.'

'What about him?'

'He'll do. You can look in on him now and again. When he comes to, let me know and I'll look him over. We've got more important work on our hands.'

So they left the hut and Mary, still cautious, looked around at the devastation. The white adobe homes standing on the edge of town had least damage. They were soot-blackened and scorched but the wooden outhouses – privies and storehouses – had gone up in flames as had a long straggling row of the poorer houses, the shacks and huts like her own. She had been one of the lucky folk with a roof still over her head.

She saw at a glance what must be done. Isaac Sloane and his daughter were already taking charge of the living and limped over to them to offer her help.

They brought the wounded and injured back to Mary's house, which was turned into a doctor's office. There, Geoff saw those who could walk in or be carried in for first aid treatment.

He was frustrated by the lack of real facilities but those he treated were grateful. They knew nothing better. If he hadn't been amongst them some of them would have died from lead poisoning or bled to death.

At the end of the day he was bone-weary. Improvization had drained his energy. He'd done things that would have made his tutor raise his hands in horror.

He sat outside Mary's hut and smoked a cigarette, something he'd become fond of since coming to America. The tobacco calmed his nerves. He was slumped down when Somerville came to him.

'You want food and a drink. Annie's been cooking all day. She's a hell of a wench, good at cooking as well as in bed!' He gave a grin and slapped Geoff on the shoulder. 'Cheer up, Doc, we're still alive!'

Geoff looked up at him and gave him a weak smile in return.

'I suppose that's the way to look at it. We're still breathing while those poor devils are out of their earthly misery!'

'Aw, come on, Doc, don't turn this into a world-shattering disaster! If you live long enough you'll face worse disasters than this! You want a drink, then you'll feel better.'

He followed Somerville down the unmade road where dark patches of blood showed. He averted his eyes as they both walked to where it seemed that all the survivors had gathered. They were crowding around an open fire. The smell of roasting pig assailed Geoff's nostrils and made his stomach churn.

Annie, still in her fine blue velvet low-necked gown, which was torn and stained, was busy doling out stew into tin plates. She'd raided what was left of Isaac Sloane's store and come up with a tolerably good meal for everyone.

Geoff saw that the whole community was working as a team. It wouldn't have happened back in Scotland. He couldn't imagine his folks rubbing shoulders with those living in the back alleys of Edinburgh.

Annie's face was white and gaunt and she'd been crying. Two of her girls had been shot down. She certainly looked her years.

'Thank you, Annie,' he said as she passed him a steaming plate. 'Are you allright?'

'Yes,' she said lifting her chin high. 'We've all got to carry on and rebuild and its no use weeping and wailing and wringing one's hands! Life's for the living. I'll miss Josie and Lucy.' Her voice broke. 'But I've got Sarah with me and she's a comfort.' She blinked away the threatened tears, and swore that she'd got a piece of grit in her eye.

Somerville brought his plate and squatted down by Geoff. Without a word he passed over his flask. Geoff took it and after a long swig, things looked brighter.

'Where's Shakeshaft and Billie Joe?'

'Helping with the burials. They'll be along soon,' Somerville answered briefly. He didn't tell Geoff they'd found the old priest suspended from his own cross above the altar of the church,

or of its further desecration. All that could wait.
'Feel better, Doc?'

'A little. That liquor of yours is better medicine than mine, it seems.'

'Now you're talking, Doc. A feller couldn't live
out here without his own elixir of life. That's
what you called them there bottles you were
toting?'

Geoff laughed.

'I'm beginning to think that city feller took
me for a greenhorn—'

'Which you were!'

'And took advantage of my ignorance. There
was a whole pack of 'em waiting at Ellis Island
for the immigrants to land. They were blood-
suckers allright and I never realized it. I thought
the man I dealt with was a kindly helpful soul
putting himself out to make me welcome in a
new land. What a fool I was!'

'Ah well, you live and learn, and you're learning fast, Doc. There'll be plenty you can do to
help folk once you find where you want to
settle. What's your plans? Me and Shakeshaft
are heading for Mexico out of danger from the
army.'

'I don't know. Maybe I should stay here and
help out. God knows, it could be as good as
anywhere.'

'Well, you'll have to make your mind up soon,
Doc. We'll be pulling out when things cool

down. We don't want to be here when the army arrives.'

The next few days passed hazily for Geoff. He tended the wounded, helped with a difficult birth brought on by the trauma of the woman seeing her husband shot in front of her eyes. Then he found himself making decisions for a people too dazed to think for themselves.

Shakeshaft and Somerville were organizing teams of men in cutting down trees and hauling them back to build new homes. Isaac Sloane was busy doling out meagre rations of foodstuffs to Annie and her women helpers, to keep the big iron pots bubbling away with bean chilli and corn mush. A clay oven had been rigged up and Annie was proving she was as good at turning out tortillas as she was in bed.

It was in the midst of all this activity that a young boy, ordered to keep watch on a high pinnacle of rock for the return of the Jayhawkers came running into the town square, his face red, his chest heaving.

'There's a cloud of dust coming towards us from the east,' he gasped.

Somerville, who'd been overseeing one of the new buildings, raised his head sharply.

'The east? Are you sure?' He'd reckoned on the newcomers riding in from the west or south.

'Yes, I'm sure,' the boy replied indignantly.

'It's a long line, like a snake and it's moving fast!'

Somerville didn't answer but went off at a run, shouting for Shakeshaft working close by.

'I think we got trouble!'

Shakeshaft downed tools and ran with him to the look-out post, and what they saw was as the boy had reported.

Somerville cursed. He'd not got his field glasses with him so could not make out the riders, but riders they were for the detail was coming in at a precise military gallop and he judged that whoever they were they would be in town in a couple of hours.

'What d'you think, Shakeshaft? They're not Indians and they're not that Jayhawker rabble.'

'You're right, boss, and they're coming at a fair lick. What we do? Leg it or stand and wait?'

'We can't leave the doc and the townsfolk. They're vulnerable if they're raiders. Maybe we should take cover and see what happens. We'll warn the men and Doc and we'll go raid Sloane's store of dynamite. If things get rough, we'll have our own little war. What d'you say?'

Shakeshaft grinned.

'Suits me fine. If it's Jayhawkers coming in, in a round-about way, we'll give 'em a surprise. If it's the army, I don't mind giving the bastards a lesson in explosives. After all, they gave me hell for being who I was!'

'Good for you!' Somerville slapped Shakeshaft

on the back. 'You're a good man, Shakeshaft and I'm proud to have you with me. Can we rely on Billie Joe?'

'I reckon not. I haven't seen him around for the last two days. Better at scouting than mopping up.'

'Well, not to worry. Maybe he's playing both ends from the middle. If that dust is from the army, chances are he's riding along with them. Maybe guiding them in and they'll know we're here!'

Shakeshaft's teeth showed in a snarl.

'If that's the case, I'll slit his throat myself!'

They scrambled down from the look-out post.

'You warn the womenfolk to get under cover with the young 'uns while I see to the men,' said Somerville harshly. 'There's a team chopping trees down. They'll have to be warned.'

He ran towards a couple of men who were struggling with the framework of a cabin, heaving at the rough logs to set them in place.

'Hey, Marvin, there's a posse coming in from the east!'

The man turned, looked at him with surprise and wiped his forehead.

'What of it? If it's the army, we'll get some help here. God knows we can do with it!'

Just then a shot rang out, the blast coming from behind Somerville. He watched Marvin collapse, spouting blood. At once there was uproar as women screamed, dragging children into any hole they could find, while the men's first reactions were to find any weapons they had at hand.

Somerville turned swiftly, expecting to see a bunch of diehard Jayhawkers wanting revenge. To his surprise and consternation he saw an Indian up on a crag, intent on aiming at someone down below. It looked like the bastard had his sights on Shakeshaft.

Somerville's reaction was immediate. The rifle in his hand came up and he took two quick shots. The Indian fell head over heels, arms flailing till he hit the ground. His scream died abruptly.

Then Somerville swung around again. Galloping hoofs seemed to come from all sides and there they were, a strong band of Cheyenne, all painted for war. At the head of them was Billy Joe, alongside a young brave sporting a chief's feathers.

Somerville cursed as he saw Billy Joe riding in. So, the dirty renegade had thrown in with the Indians and led them to Shakeshaft, for no doubt he was the target for this little caper.

But there was no time for bitter recriminations or blaming himself for not guessing the real reason why Billy Joe had joined them. He saw the doc come out of the makeshift hospital to see what the commotion was.

'Get down!' he yelled. He flung himself down behind a pile of timber and then turned to fire at the oncoming Indians.

He took Billy Joe in the throat, then, as the Cheyenne came screaming in, he shot the young chieftain who was launching himself on Shakeshaft, who, because of his previous wound, was not so quick on the draw.

The raid was over in a few minutes but it seemed hours. One of the painted braves yelled a sharp command when he saw their chieftain fall to the ground, and the whole pack turned and galloped away in the direction from which they'd come.

Somerville could hardly believe the devastation caused in those few minutes. Five men lay dead or dying, along with Billy Joe and three Cheyenne, one of whom was still groaning. Shakeshaft strode over to him, hoping to recognize him. He squatted and rubbed paint from the man's face and as he did so, a hand came up holding a knife aiming at Shakeshaft's neck. It was a weak attempt, the last defiance of a man who was dying.

With a snarl, Shakeshaft wrested it from the man and plunged it into his heart. Then stood up, threw the bloodstained blade on to the man's chest and walked away, his face tight and angry.

Geoff, white-faced and shaken by the quick-fire raid, hastened to examine the bodies, hoping that some might be still alive. It was to no avail, they were all dead. He gave a great sigh. Here was more heartbreak for the womenfolk left behind. He felt helpless, inadequate. He had so much to learn and he thought he would never get used to the sudden violence in this land that was still a mystery to him.

The only thing he could do was to get his hands dirty. He had to help dig graves along with the other able-bodied men, and when not needed by the wounded, go help saw down trees and build new homes.

He had to put his calling on one side, to become as the other frontiersmen were, to use his own special expertise when needed but it wasn't the most important thing in his life now. He was just beginning to realize that to survive out here in the wilderness one had to be an expert in all skills. Being a doctor was just a bonus.

Somerville was astonished when he volunteered to dig graves.

'Are you sure, Doc? You're going to get those hands of yours a mite blistered!'

Geoff felt a kind of shame.

'Look, I'm an able-bodied man,' he said brusquely. 'I'm just as capable of digging as the next man. Maybe I wasn't born to a shovel but I can do my share!'

Somerville shrugged. 'OK, Doc, but it's mighty hard work, The ground's hard and we dig deep to protect the bodies from being dug up again by the big cats!'

So Geoff took a shovel and found Somerville was right. His back ached and his tender hands were soon sore but manfully he carried on without complaint. What other men could do, so could he.

They had buried two bodies. Already the flies were buzzing around in the heat of the day. They not only attacked the bloodstained bodies but were attracted by the sweat of the men working over the graves. Geoff straightened up to ease his aching back and to wipe the sweat from his forehead. He needed a drink badly and ice-cool river water was what he wanted.

He took his empty canteen down to the river, filled it, then sluiced water over his head. He revelled in the shock of it.

Then, as he turned to come back up the bank, he paused, for riding into the square was a troop of soldiers headed by an officer who must surely be a captain. Geoff's heart lifted. Thank God for the army! Now they would have some protection!

He was ready to run forward with a greeting when he frowned, for something was very wrong. He saw Somerville turn to run and then Geoff remembered what Somerville had told him. He was now a discredited officer and a deserter!

He saw the captain spur his horse and gallop after Somerville who was heading for the trees. The captain lunged forward over his horse's neck and using his riding crop, caught Somerville across the shoulders. Geoff swore.

He saw Shakeshaft spring at the man on horseback, but two soldiers leapt into action and Shakeshaft was rolled on the ground. Two rifles pointed at his heart.

'Somerville,' roared the man on horseback, 'Give yourself up or my men will shoot the 'breed!'

Geoff saw all the fight leave Somerville. His hung head and bowed shoulders said it all. He saw Somerville look up at the captain who gave him a malicious smile.

'I'll come quietly, Captain, but let Shakeshaft go. He's not army personel.'

'Like hell we will! You're in no position to bargain, Somerville. I'm taking you both back. After all, the bastard engineered your escape. I never approved of your friendship with the swine. No true American would consort with an Indian, even less so with a 'breed!'

'He was a good loyal scout!'

'Loyal, my eye! He had a foot in both camps! No doubt he supplied information to the

Cheyenne like he supplied us with information about them!'

Somerville stared up at the officer in futile rage. They had never got on. Captain Hawkswell had been one of the officers sitting in judgment at the court martial and his voice had been loudest in condemning him.

'You were always a bastard, Hawkswell! It's a wonder one of your own men hasn't stuck a knife in your back before now!'

Captain Hawkswell reached down and slapped Somerville's cheek, knocking him backwards. Geoff saw blood as Somerville's teeth bit into the flesh of his cheek.

There was a rising gasp of protest from the gravediggers. The soldiers turned to hold them back, rifles raised to shoot.

This was Geoff's chance, as the soldiers had their backs to him. He sprinted across the ground, anger making him oblivious to danger. He'd show the bastard!

Before Hawkswell knew what was happening he was dragged off his horse. Geoff aimed a punch at his head. The man went sprawling and Geoff stood over him, fists at the ready. He'd show the arrogant swine just how they fought back home. He took another swing as Hawkswell scrambled to his feet, his face dark with anger.

The soldiers holding Shakeshaft to the ground turned to see what the commotion was about.

Shakeshaft jumped to his feet, snatching both men's rifles before they realized what was happening. Then, holding one weapon between his legs, he fanned around at the watching soldiers.

'The first man to move, gets it!' the ferocious snarl on Shakeshaft's face paralysed them all.

It was a fight that was retold many times in the years to come. How Doctor Geoff Potterson played cat and mouse with the captain, dancing in and out of reach, placing stinging punches that hurt but did no real damage. Even amongst the soldiers there were those who applauded what this man was doing, for Captain Hawkswell was not a popular officer.

They saw that Geoff was out to give long-drawn-out punishment. They watched the bruised cheeks blackened and one eye closed. They saw the deliberate placing of blows that would hurt the most. They watched Hawkswell stagger around throwing punches that rarely found a target but wore himself out.

They concluded that this Britisher used an unusual skill. It was no barroom roughhouse, but a masterly art of deliberate punishment. When Geoff thought the man had had enough, he gave him the final perfect punch on the jaw, which lifted Hawkswell off his feet and sent him sprawling on his back, out cold.

There was a cheering from the townsfolk and

mutterings from the soldiers. Hawkswell's sergeant looked at Geoff who was rubbing his knuckles. He looked at him with respect.

'Sir, what should I do with him?'

Geoff smiled.

'Throw a bucket of water over him. What else?'

The sergeant grinned and squatted by the officer.

'Sir . . . wake up, sir!' But there was no response so Sergeant Dobbs heaved him up and over his shoulder and took him down to the river.

Geoff watched them go, then turned his attention to Somerville, who was mopping the cut on his cheek.

'You allright, Somerville? I'll look at that cut of yours.'

'Goddammit, Doc, don't make such a fuss! It's only a cut! I'm fine. You perked me up no end when you went for him. The best medicine in the world! I must hand it to you, Doc, you know how to use your fists!' He held out his hand for Geoff to shake. 'You're a right buddy after all.' Then he looked at Geoff's hand when he saw him wince. 'Jesus! Holy Mother Mary! I reckon I should be binding up your hands! I've never known hands take such punishment. Better use a gun next time!'

Geoff smiled ruefully.

'Maybe you're right, but boxing comes as second nature. I think I've got to rethink my life and forget the past. It's gun law out here. No time for honourable pastimes!'

Somerville shook his head as Geoff walked away to the improvised hospital to attend to his hands. There goes what he would describe as a perfect English gent. What a goddamn waste, turning a gent into a fast-gun, jack-of-all-trades survival expert, who could live off the land. It would take some doing but to live, Doc Geoff Potterson would have to come down to a frontiersman's level and that meant drinking to blot out the past and whoring around for such as they could not afford the luxury of women of their own.

SEVEN

Somerville wasn't the only man to watch Geoff disappear into his little hospital. Shakeshaft drew on a cigarette, still marvelling at the doc's prowess with his fists. He'd certainly turned a sticky situation into a humiliating defeat for that bastard, Hawkswell. Serve the scumbag right! Shakeshaft had never liked him. He only wished the doc had gone all the way and killed him.

Now that the fracas was over, his own instincts kicked in. No one seemed to be in charge of the newcomers unless you could call the sergeant in charge and he was dunking Hawkswell in the river and no further orders had been issued.

So, taking a last puff of his cigarette and stubbing it out with his toe, he made his way across to Somerville.

'I reckon you'd better take command of these here fellers. That there sergeant knows shit!'

Somerville shook his head.

'I'm a deserter. I'm no longer eligible.' He

spoke with sadness and regret.

'You prided yourself on your career, didn't you, boss?'

'Yes, it was my life. It proved to me that my father was wrong. He reckoned I was a no-good piece of trash because I questioned his teachings. I sent him a letter when I made lieutenant. I hope he choked on it!' He laughed bitterly. 'Now, I'm up shit creek because of that damned Hawkswell!'

'We can still go to Mexico together, boss, and we can take the doc with us when all this is over. You could still give orders for the troop to move out!'

'I'll think about it.'

'Meanwhile I think I'll go stretch my horse's legs and take a look around for any lurking Cheyenne. I'm a bit sensitive where they're concerned. They never give up!'

Somerville sighed as he watched Shakeshaft go for his horse and ride away. He was in a dilemma. He knew he couldn't give orders but he wasn't going to let Hawkswell take him away tied to his horse like any common criminal.

Shakeshaft rode the high country, stopping now and again to rake the distant hills and lower valley for any indication that the Cheyenne were hiding out, waiting for the moment when the troops left to make another raid. There was also the risk of Jayhawkers coming up from the south in revenge for their lost herds. Hardly likely but there could be a few hotheads ready for a scrap.

It was several hours before he saw the smudge of dust on one of the main trails. He could even see it without his glasses. Focusing his glasses he could see that it was another army troop and with them were a bunch of cowboys. It looked as if the ranchers and the army had joined up and were coming at a fair good pace. Usually the troops moved slowly and deliberately but these sons of bitches were galloping and that usually meant they knew exactly where they were going and in a hurry!

It didn't take a genius to know where they were heading. They were coming into town!

Shakeshaft dropped his glasses, they hung loose by a strap around his neck. No time to put them carefully away in his saddlebag. He jerked on the horse's rein, kicked his heels and turned to go back the way he'd come. Fortunately he knew the nearly extinct Indian trails and so could take a short cut and beat that platoon back to the small settlement. He could warn Somerville that there was a major out there hunting for them both. Wryly, he wondered at the importance the top brass seemed to place upon bringing a disgraced lieutenant and a scout back to justice.

There was no time to lose! If he and

Somerville wanted to escape they must do it at once!

Shakeshaft got a shock when he arrived back at the community. They were surrounded by Cheyenne intent on reclaiming the body of their young chief and another couple of braves.

He heard the intense firing well before he came into view. God's curse on the red devils, he muttered under his breath. Now what to do? The swine must have attacked only a few hours after he'd left. But as he moved cautiously closer he saw that the Cheyenne were facing far more fire than they'd anticipated for the soldiers were dotted behind anything that would protect them and they'd manoeuvred into a makeshift ring around the partly built cabins. He smiled. That was one of Somerville's tactics. Make use of every scrap of cover, whether it was a tuft of grass or a boulder.

He waited, helpless, tying his horse well away from danger and then went, Indian fashion, to watch and wait.

Then, hearing a rustle in the brush, he bellied forward, taking his time. There before him was an Indian. He watched him for a few minutes and recognized the muscled back and the ornaments on his arms. He waited, heart pounding until the man turned his head and yes, he knew the son of a bitch as one of those who had condemned Kalia and his son. He remembered

139

him as a bullying youth, when he was a boy and wanted Kalia for himself.

Anger engulfed him. A red mist seemed to envelop him. He sprang to his feet and leapt like a puma for the Indian's back but some sixth sense made the Indian turn. Recognition sprang into his eyes as he tried to parry Shakeshaft's onslaught. Teeth bared and snarling, he closed with Shakeshaft and then the silent struggle took place.

Both men were lithe and fit but Shakeshaft had the advantage of rage and the need for revenge for what had happened to Kalia and their son.

Their bodies entwined as they both tried to find strangleholds. First one and then the other was on top and they rolled down a steep incline. They were well out of sight of what was going on in the settlement.

Shakeshaft wanted to curse the man now fighting for his life but he knew he had to save his wind and his strength to overcome the powerful hold the brave had on one wrist. They strained and sweated; Shakeshaft suffered a bite on his shoulder while he vainly tried to bring a knee up to connect with the man's genitals.

With a mighty effort, Shakeshaft broke the man's hold on his wrist and managed to land two jabs to the head that rocked his opponent backwards. Then with a snarl, Shakeshaft was on him.

His hands closed about the bulging neck ... there would be no short sharp stab of a knife to end this man's life. He would die hard ...

His eyes bulging, his throat giving choking grunts, the man on the ground tried to heave himself upwards but to no avail. Each time his head was rocked back against the hard earth. Slowly the face turned puce, the eyes still glared their murderous hate until the light in them started to fade. Then the face turned black and the tongue protruded. Shakeshaft felt the spirit leave the body.

He found he could not relax his hands. They were as if fused to the man's neck. He lay crouched over the corpse, gasping for breath and as his heart slowed its pounding he felt the exultant joy of victory. Without thinking, he threw back his head and whooped his defiance to all who would hear him. The Cheyenne victory yell came naturally, taught him by his stepfather, Chief Shakeshaft himself.

Down in the settlement the whoop was heard. The Cheyenne, still fighting, all thought it was their dead chief spurring them on and Somerville, who heard the call, was convinced another wave of Cheyenne was coming in. Things were looking desperate.

Not too far away, the major leading the troop raised a hand for the men to halt. He and they heard the last of the spine-chilling scream;

quickly he gave the order to advance at a gallop.

The men were strung out in fours and they covered the ground at a cracking pace.

Somerville rallied the troops and the towns-folk for another onslaught by the Indians. This time the Cheyenne came on regardless of the heavy fire. It was as if they didn't care whether they lived or died.

But their savage attack was taking its toll. The doc was busy in between bursts of gunfire, patching up wounds. The dead had to lie where they fell.

The air smelled of gunpowder, blood and excrement and the screams of women and children and those of the oncoming Indians blended with the staccato sounds of gunfire.

Then Geoff raised his head and paused in the act of tying up a bandage for a soldier. Their eyes met.

'Did I hear right? Or was that the sound of a bugle?' asked Geoff of the man.

The man grinned.

'Too damn right! You're not hearing things. I heard it too!'

Geoff left him and went to stand at the door of his hospital hut to see what was happening. It was then he heard the deep-throated cheering and watched spellbound as the army troop, with the Stars and Stripes flag flying at the head, came thundering down the slope towards the little township. Miraculously there wasn't an Indian to be seen or heard! They had retreated into the bushes and were probably half a mile away by now.

Geoff wanted to cry. The relief was so great that his legs trembled and he felt his strength leave him. It was hunger, he told himself firmly and staggered outside to go and greet the newcomers.

Major Carruthers stepped down from his horse after giving his sergeant orders to deploy his men around the town and beat the bushes for lurking Indians. He strode over to Somerville and looked him up and down.

'Who's in charge here? You seem to be having fun and games!'

His keen eyes took in the state of the men and knew it had been a long battle.

'We heard the war-whoop and came as fast as we could. Are you the man in charge?'

Somerville coughed.

'Not exactly, sir.'

'What does that mean?'

'Well, sir, Captain Hawkswell was indisposed, so I stood in for him, sir!'

'So you were in charge!'

'Just for that skirmish, sir!'

The major frowned.

'I'm looking for a Lieutenant Somerville . . .'

He was rudely interrupted by a very damp

143

staggering figure with a swollen eye and bruised chin, coming out from the shelter of some rocks where his sergeant had flung him.

'Hold that man! He's my prisoner! Goddammit, I'll get him back to Fort Blaine if it's the last thing I do! Him and his son of a bitch buddy, the murdering doctor and the 'breed if I can find him!' Hawkswell, full of anger stared at the major and only then taking in the officer's status added: 'Sir!' He saluted quickly as he swayed before the officer.

'Are you Captain Hawkswell?'

'Yes sir, of the twelfth division.'

'And who's this man who stood in for you while you were . . . er . . . indisposed?'

'Lieutenant Somerville, or should I say, ex-Lieutenant Somerville.' Hawkswell grinned crookedly because of his swollen jaw.

The major slapped his thigh with his whip and stared pensively at the captain. Then he said quietly:

'I must inform you, Captain, that Lieutenant Somerville is no longer a wanted man. I understand he is responsible for preventing those Mexican cattle from overrunning our state. Those cattle would have infected the stock in this area with their ticks and we all know what that would have meant.' He turned to Somerville and held out his hand. 'Why didn't you tell me you were Somerville? I'm proud to shake your hand!

It must have been quite an enterprise going down into that pass and calculating where to set the charges for the explosives. You were an experienced explosives officer, I take it.'

'Yes, sir, during the war I had much experience.'

'Good. My colonel is seeking an experienced officer to be in a charge of the arsenal ... the last officer died during an explosion. Would you be willing to take the post? You would not go back to Fort Blaine.'

Somerville was startled. He had already made plans with Shakeshaft and there was the doctor to consider. He hesitated and the major grew impatient.

'Well, man, what is it to be?'

Somerville was about to answer when a rider could be seen and heard coming racing into the settlement. Somerville grinned as he watched Shakeshaft waving his hat and whooping like a Cheyenne.

Geoff came out to watch and he too grinned and waved back.

The major stared hard at the incoming man.

'Who in hell's that?'

'Sir, that's the best scout the army ever had. That's Shakeshaft, sir.' A grinning Somerville waved in return.

The major was quick to assess the situation between the men.

'Would you consider the post if the scout was hired too?'

Geoff heard the question and he too looked at Somerville. What now?

'I can't speak for Shakeshaft, sir. He is a wanted man by the Cheyenne and lives from day to day.'

'Then how about you? Does the post tempt you?'

Somerville held out his hand.

'Yes sir. I never wanted to leave the service. I guess I'm an army man through and through!'

'Good. Now we wait and see what this man of yours decides to do.'

Shakeshaft stood up in the stirrups for the remaining few yards, gave a last whoop and then drew up, his horse rearing on his back legs. It was a spectacular show-off in proper Cheyenne style. Shakeshaft would never forget his mother's people even as he tried to live amongst white folk.

Geoff watched, admiring Shakeshaft's skill on a horse. He knew he would never come up to that standard. Then he noticed Captain Hawkswell standing ignored, growing more angry every minute.

He watched while the major's and Somerville's attention was concentrating on Shakeshaft who stood sweaty and jubilant before them. He saw Hawkswell's hand reach for his

146

army Colt and saw that Somerville's back must be the target. Geoff lunged forward in one of his old football tackles learned during his university years, just as the man's gunhand came up. The gun fired, the bullet was deflected into the air, and Geoff rolled the captain over. He sat down hard on him, his teeth gritted murderously.

'You bastard!' he grated, and held the squirming man down as Somerville and the major turned to see what the gunshot and scuffle was all about.

Two soldiers standing by helped Geoff to his feet and hauled the captain upright. The man breathed heavily, his eyes glittering, but he remained silent.

Geoff nursed his bruised hands; the pain was now very evident.

'Doc, what happened?' Somerville came over to him. 'Your hands!'

Geoff grinned wryly.

'The goddamn swine was going to backshoot you, Somerville. He's mad and should be shut away!'

Major Carruthers heard the words and nodded at the men holding Hawkswell.

'Put him in chains and we'll take him back to Fort Blaine!'

'No!' The stentorian yell ripped through the air, startling the bystanders. Before anyone could

147

react, Hawkswell snatched a gun from one of the soldiers holding him. As they tried to wrest it from him, he turned it on himself and a bullet tore through his brain.

For a moment all stood aghast, then the major, showing no emotion, turned away with a muttered order to his sergeant.

'Dispose of the body, Sergeant. We've got other work to do!'

Guards were set at points around the township, a patrol was sent out to scour the country for hostiles and the army cooks got busy and helped the womenfolk of the town to prepare meals.

They stayed on guard all night. Then, next morning, Major Carruthers requested the presence of the scout known as Shakeshaft.

'I'm sure Lieutenant Somerville has already explained that he is now free of all charges and has agreed to a new post. What I want to know is, are you willing to go with him as his chief scout?'

Shakeshaft drew a deep breath. There was a great sadness in him. It would be hard to take leave of the man he'd called boss. But there was no way he could remain as a scout. He had to go and make a new life in Mexico away from all Cheyenne vengeance. He knew he was only living on borrowed time if he remained with the army. Someday, the Cheyenne would get lucky.

Somerville saw the pain in him.

'Shakeshaft, I shall understand if you don't want to come with me,' he began.

Shakeshaft shook his head.

'I *do* want to come with you, but I cannot! You know the reason why! It's not possible!'

Somerville shook his head while Major Carruthers looked puzzled. Somerville explained as briefly as possible.

'Sir, with respect to Shakeshaft here, I must tell you he is of mixed blood and against all Cheyenne rules he took a Cheyenne woman as wife. They had a child, and when Shakeshaft had to leave her during the war, she went back to the tribe. They killed her and the boy and swore vengeance for his defilement of her. Shakeshaft lives from day to day. At any time he could be slain!'

Major Carruthers coughed. He was appalled.

'Is this true?'

Shakeshaft nodded.

'Then all I can do is shake your hand and wish you well. You may draw whatever rations you need for your continuing journey into Mexico.'

They shook hands and, to Somerville's surprise, Shakeshaft saluted him. Until now, Shakeshaft had never saluted an officer, figuring that as he wasn't actually in the army there was no need to kowtow to anybody.

Sadly Geoff watched the little ceremony. It was going to be a wrench to see the 'breed ride away.

149

He gave a start when Major Carruthers turned to him.

'Doctor, we need doctors with your skill in the army. What about joining forces with us? Your recruitment would only be a matter of signing a paper. Will you come back to Fort Blaine with us?'

Geoff took a deep breath. It was an honour indeed but . . . He looked about him at the half-built homes, the devastation that had to be cleared away. He saw the tough survivors making the best of what was left. He thought of the women . . . He couldn't leave them.

'Sir, I'm honoured by your invitation but I'm sorry, I must turn it down. My place is here, helping to rebuild what has been destroyed. I am not only a doctor, I am also a man and I reckon it is my duty to help these people in all ways. I am sorry. I shall not ride with you.'

The major nodded.

'I am disappointed but I understand and all good luck to you.' He turned to his sergeant. 'Sergeant, order the men to be ready to pull out at dawn!'

That night Geoff sat up late around the camp-fire talking to the men closest to him in this new land. It was the parting of the ways. He felt very emotional when they drank a toast to each other in the glow of the fire. They were all a little drunk when they eventually turned in.

150

'It's been good to know you, Doc,' Somerville slurred, 'but you've got to learn to be a better rider. You're still clumsy.'

'And you'd better get some practice in with the gun and the knife,' hiccuped Shakeshaft. Then he said softly: 'Thank you both for being my friends. It's been an honour to know you both.'

And Geoff Potterson, one-time Edinburgh Universty student said softly:

'And thank you both for educating me!' Then they hit the sack.

EIGHT

Five years on, Dr Geoff Potterson sat on his veranda smoking his pipe and watching the setting sun send streaks of gold and red across the sky. It would be another good day tomorrow.

He never tired of the view in front of him. The newly built wooden houses interspersed among the still-blackened and sooty adobe houses and the new hotel and the two saloons along with Annie's new abode always attracted much coming and going. Further down the straggling street was Isaac Sloane's new store and the hostelry. Yes, the town had grown much in the last few years, especially since Annie had imported a batch of new girls.

Occasionally Geoff wondered why he didn't marry. He had been tempted a few times to pay court to some respectable female but after knowing Annie and her girls, respectable females seemed so meek and colourless. He couldn't imagine living the rest of his life with a dull wife.

He sighed. Sometimes after a long day when perhaps he'd driven miles in his buggy cart ... he'd never become easy on horseback ... he would have appreciated a warm tender wife to come home to.

So he made do with meals at Bessie's Eatery and whatever he needed at Annie's and then sat and dreamed on his own veranda listening to the creaking shingle swinging above his door.

He had a lot to be thankful for, he reckoned. The menfolk of the town helped him build his home and an extension. He now had a small hospital with a six-bed ward and a consulting-room and office.

He wondered what his father would think of his primitive existence. No doubt he would raise his hands in horror at the thought of his son living in such conditions.

But what the hell! The old man would never know. He also would never know that Geoff's patients were his friends too. That was something his father would never have allowed. There were rigid guidelines back home about the relationship between doctors and patients. Here in the West all men were survivors and helped each other. His father would never have understood that.

He stood up and stretched, thinking about those other close friends, Somerville and Shakeshaft. He often wondered how they got on in their new lives. Maybe one day, one or both might come riding back. It would be like old times and they'd celebrate. He smiled at the thought.

In the meantime, he would wander down the street, greeting friends and patients alike and he would go and visit Annie and her girls. He was sure of a welcome there. . . .

Far away in Washington DC, Somerville gazed into the mirror as he adjusted his new uniform. He was clean-shaven. The barber had done a good job on both face and hair. He looked what he was, colonel-in-chief of the newly formed Explosives Division. He smiled at his reflection. Not bad for a man once wanted by the army for desertion. He straightened his shoulders, then took his cap from his batman and settled it on his heat at rakish angle.

'Satisfied, Briggs?'

Briggs looked him up and down.

'Yes sir! Not a piece of fluff anywhere, sir!'

'Good. Now I'll be off. Even a colonel can't keep a president waiting!'

The batman grinned.

'Good luck, sir! Hope you enjoy the evening!'

'Oh, yes, I'll enjoy it. I understand all the unmarried ladies in Washington will be at the reception!'

*

Shakeshaft leaned on his hoe and grinned as his plump wife, heavy with their second child, came across the field. She was bringing him bread and some goat cheese and a jug of home-made beer. Their son, Juan, a sturdy boy going on three, clung to her skirt, his fat legs struggling to keep up with her.

He crouched down when they came near and held out his arms. The child ran to him and he was swung up into the air, the boy wriggling and giggling. Shakeshaft put him down gently, went to Maria and took the jug and food from her.

'You shouldn't have come yourself. It's far too far for you at this time. You should have sent your sister!'

They sat down together, Maria gently panting.

'I wanted to come. I need the exercise and the baby kicks so much. Maybe tomorrow will be the day!'

She looked at him with love, and blessed the day he'd come riding in to her father's hacienda, bringing with him her young brother, the apple of her father's eye, whom he'd found beaten up a few miles from the hacienda.

The boy had been left for dead. Shakeshaft had revived him enough to tell him where to take him and that had been the start of a new life for Shakeshaft.

After weeks of nursing, the boy had survived and a grateful father had welcomed Shakeshaft as one of his own. He'd watched tolerantly as the stranger and his eldest daughter, Maria, first became friends and then it became evident that a marriage must take place before passion spilled over.

Don Rodriguez took matters into his own hands and bluntly asked Shakeshaft his intentions. He hinted that there would be no objection to marriage and that he would treat Shakeshaft as his own son.

So now he had a loving wife and a second child on the way. Sometimes late at night he would think of Kalia and their child and he would pray for them. Then he would turn over, and put a hand out and feel Maria's soft body sleeping beside him. He was content.

Mexico! This was now his land. He could see no reason why he should ever move on again. He'd come home.